MW01502674

M	166-83
	Mitchell, Gladys

AUTHOR

HERE LIES GLORIA MUNDY

TITLE

DATE DUE

Matthews			
Russo			
Handel			
Scaley			
OCT 9 - '91			

HERE LIES GLORIA MUNDY

Here Lies
GLORIA MUNDY

Gladys Mitchell

St. Martin's Press
New York

Library of Congress Cataloging in Publication Data

Mitchell, Gladys, 1901-
   Here lies Gloria Mundy.

   I. Title.
PR6025.I832H4   1983   823'.912   83-2924
ISBN 0-312-36986-7

First published in Great Britain by Michael Joseph Ltd.

First U.S. Edition

10 9 8 7 6 5 4 3 2 1

To
QUENTIN

who, like St Joan, has accepted
the burdens which are too heavy
for the rest of us

CONTENTS

1
A Case in the Papers

At school I always insisted that my first name was Colin. This is an acceptable name among boys. My baptismal name of Corin is not, although why this should be I don't know. Can one consonant make such a difference?

The trouble is that I have a twin sister whom my father was determined should be christened Corinna. My mother wanted her called Oenone, so, to settle the matter, they agreed upon Corin and Corinna, much to my youthful discomfiture. Talk about 'Hello, twins!'

When I got to university, however, I realised that it was no bad thing to have a name which, so far as I know, has nothing but literary connections, so I reverted to Corin and have become, in a modest way, part of the contemporary scribal scene. That is to say, I earn my living as a writer under the name of Corin Stratford. Stratford is not my patronymic, but nowadays most people use it, as I have made it clear that it is in my professional interests that my name should be publicised as much as possible.

I was determined not to tie myself down to a nine-to-five job, but neither was I prepared to do a Mr Micawber and wait for something to turn up. My father was willing to continue my small allowance – as much as he could possibly afford – for a couple of years after I left college, but after that I had to fend for myself. Fair enough, I thought. I had faith in myself and decided to make my name the appendage to a modicum of fame even if I starved while this was happening.

'Does the road wind uphill all the way?' asked Christina Rossetti. Well, it certainly did for me, but, after a hard slog, the way up has eased to a gentle gradient and at the beginning of this year I found myself, if not affluent, at least able to afford a small flat in Baker Street instead of being in digs, and to take a holiday when and where I chose.

I had been in the flat for only a fortnight when I read about the murder of a young woman who had been living in one room in the neighbourhood of Earls Court.

I had done some freelance work for *Dawn Chorus*, the paper which carried the fullest coverage of the murder, so I telephoned and was told (as I had expected) that the story was being covered by the paper's own reporters. However, I was also told when and where the inquest was to be held, and I decided to attend it, since it seemed to me, judging by the account given in the papers, that, after a lapse of time and some artful manipulation of the facts, a lucrative bit of fiction might evolve. It was a long-term proposition, but I am a patient man and so much inured to delays, frustrations and disappointments that I have become something of a philosopher and content to bide my time.

The coroner's court was full, for any chance of obtaining free entertainment is not to be missed. I managed to get a seat next to one of the *Dawn Chorus* reporters just before the coroner got to work. Compared with the luridly written-up account of the murder in the newspaper, however, the proceedings were colourless and dull. Evidence of identity and the medical evidence were dealt with and the police then asked for an adjournment.

Assisted far more by the account in *Dawn Chrous* than by the court proceedings, I roughed out a story as soon as I got back to my flat after a pub lunch in the Earls Court Road, and then I put my notes aside to ferment and then mature.

The story was commonplace enough. The murdered woman had spent some time in America, according to the sleazy old party who gave evidence of identity, and had been lodging in London for a matter of six years. During that time she had had visitors of both sexes, some of whom claimed to be relatives, although the landlady did not believe this.

The landlady had no rules against visitors. (This I got from the newspaper. It was not mentioned at the inquest.) They were, according to her, all of them respectable people, quiet, well-behaved, never stopping more than a couple of hours and certainly never staying the night. The reporter who recorded this had managed, with cunning skill, to query most of it without actually appearing to cast doubt on the landlady's assertions. I am sure he was worth his pay. I knew his work, and admired it, although I could not have emulated it. Suffice to say that, however close to the wind his paper sailed, so far it had never been involved in an action for libel, although there were rumours of sums having exchanged hands out of court.

When I learned that the murdered girl had had a baby with her when she arrived and that the child had been taken into care only after the death of the mother, I discounted the *Dawn Chorus* innuendoes. Ladies of doubtful virtue do not discourage their clients by having to get up in the night to soothe or feed an infant, nor do they want a six-year-old sharing the bedroom. Also, as the reporter, to his credit, did not fail to point out, the child had never been neglected or ill-treated.

One item which the newspaper had got hold of was that the girl was on her way to find out more about a situation as chambermaid in a hotel near Brighton when she met death. How she had come to hear of the post remained a mystery. The landlady thought she had heard of it through a friend, not by reading an advertisement, but there was no proof of this, or of who the friend might be.

From that journey she never came back. When she did not return, the landlady took it for granted that she had been given the job and had begun work, but after a day or two, during which the girl had not come for the child, the landlady began to wonder, especially as one or two people came to enquire after the girl and she could tell them nothing. Then a young reporter somehow got hold of the landlady's story and asked for the address of the hotel, but all that she could supply was its name. He went to the police. He knew the London to Brighton roads very well, he told them, but had never seen a hotel, pub or roadhouse with the name the landlady had given him.

A few days later the body was found washed up near Hastings. It had not drowned; there were no signs of sexual assault; death had resulted from stab wounds, one of which had penetrated the heart.

The police began their usual painstaking work and the papers soon dropped the case. Shorn of any salacious details, it made dull reading after its first impact. I myself was somewhat disappointed in it as it stood, but I set aside my notes again, with the reflection gained from Rabindranath Tagore that 'Truth in her dress finds facts too tight. In fiction she moves with ease.'

I never wrote the story because, merely through a chance meeting with a friend I had not seen for years, I was caught up in a far better one. All the same, I did go to see the landlady.

'You'll have to pay me for my time and trouble,' she said. 'I'm sick of giving you lot something for nothing. Show me a couple of quid and I'll show you her room, what I have not yet let, and I'll answer your questions up to a quarter of an hour, my time being money.'

'I'll skip the bedroom,' I said. 'That ought to be worth at least another five minutes of your time.' I gave her one pound and showed her the other, to be handed to her when our conversation was finished.

'You might as well be one of them mean-fisted coppers,' she grumbled; but she answered my questions and received her money well within the agreed time.

'You say she was after a job in a hotel. Did she have a job before that?'

'Bits of charring. I reckon, though, as she got bits of money from America, where she come from.'

'What makes you think so?'

'She got letters regular with postal orders in 'em.'

'How do you know that they came from America?'

'I don't know it. She always got to the front door before I did, to pick up the post.'

'If you know the letters contained postal orders, I still wonder what makes you think they came from the United States. Dollar bills or something in the nature of a cheque would be more likely.'

'That 'ud mean a bank. She never went to no bank, only to the post office.'

'You followed her, then?'

'No. I wanted to buy a stamp for me own letter to my boy what's serving the Queen in Germany, didn't I?'

'Did she ever stay out at nights?'

'She'd have been out of here P D Q if she had. This is a respectable house I'd have you to know.'

So that was that, and my notes remained unused.

2
Chance Encounter

When I ran into Hardie Keir McMaster after a lapse of seven years it was at one of the more unlikely places, for it was outside the south door of a church. There had not been a wedding or a funeral; neither was it a Sunday, so I could only conclude that he was there for the same purpose as I was. This was to take a look at the church itself, a most surprising thing for him to do. At college he had been one of our 'hearties' with, so far as anybody knew, no interest in either art or architecture.

As well as being a freelance journalist, I am a novelist and biographer. With regard to the first, I look hopefully for commissioned articles and can supply these on any subject covered by the *Encyclopaedia Britannica*, but for the other two I please myself. At the time I had just published my third novel. My biography of Horace Walpole was still selling, and the royalties had just come to hand, so I was taking a little holiday, 'resting' as actors call it, and that morning I had driven in my car to Herefordshire to look at Kilpeck church.

Kilpeck church is unique. I had heard of it from friends and had seen photographs of its south door. I was prepared for the south door, but not to see McMaster standing in front of it. I was more than surprised, but I could not mistake that massive six feet three, those mighty shoulders, the firmly planted feet and, still less, that Viking thatch of yellow hair. I went up and thumped him on the back.

It was an ill-judged act. He swung round and nearly knocked me flying. However, he collected me, planted me in front of him, held me at arms' length and said, 'Well, I'm damned. Just the very man!'

'How are you, Hara-kiri?' I asked. He had been given the title at college. He had played prop forward for us and some wit had christened him with a joke on his first names of Hardie Keir because it was alleged to be tantamount to committing suicide if you tackled him on the field. Off it, a sucking dove might have envied him and even striven to emulate him, for he was normally the gentlest and most amiable of creatures.

'Corin Stratford, by heaven!' he shouted. 'What on earth are you doing here, you old son of a mermaid?'

'Taking a photograph of the south door of this church, when you move your great carcase out of the way,' I said. Unmistakeably of its period, the south doorway of Kilpeck church nevertheless bears some striking and unusual features. Like many late Norman doorways, it is extensively decorated, and among the decorations are two warriors wearing trousers, Phrygian caps, and tunics of chain mail. I had read that the whole doorway is a representation of this sinful world of lust and strife, but it also holds a promise of better things to come, for in the concentric double tympanum arch is the Tree of Life, and on the jamb a writhing serpent is shown, head downwards in defeat.

There is a suggestion of the Saxon origin of the church in the style of some of the carvings, but even more obvious is the Celtic influence. Moreover, on the west wall of the church I had seen gargoyles in stone which could only have derived from the carved wooden prows of Viking ships, so the church is an epitome of local history.

'Let's walk round,' I said. 'There's a corbel-table underneath the eaves. There are birds and beasts and human heads. There is even a sheila-ma-gig.'

'You mean a thingummy-jig,' said McMaster.

'No, I don't. I mean a sheila-ma-gig. She's a rather rude lady who appears on some Irish churches. My guess is that she represents something fairly unspeakable from the Book of Revelations. Anyway, compare her with the crude Australian term "sheila", meaning a woman and used, I always think, in a derogatory sense. After I've identified her, if I can, I'm going inside the church. There's a notable chancel arch. After one has looked at these warriors and the serpent, and has seen the lion and the dragon fighting each other as depicted on this doorway, the chancel arch promises the peace of heaven, so that the church preaches a sermon in stone.'

'See you later, then,' he said. 'I'm going to look at the gravestones. I collect curious epitaphs.'

I laughed. 'I know one or two,' I said.

> ' "Mary Ann has gone to rest,
>   Safe at last on Abram's breast,
>   Which may be fine for Mary Ann,
>   But sure is tough on Abraham." '

He laughed, too.

'That's apocryphal,' he said, 'and, anyway, I know it.'

'All right, then. What about this one?

> "Here lies that old liar Ned,
>   But he can't lie because he's dead,
>   For now he lies on heaven's shore,
>   Where he don't need to lie no more." '

'Where did you get that?'

'From a chap in a pub in Bristol.'

'It's difficult to get them authenticated,' said McMaster, 'when they're only given you by word of mouth. I got a beauty in East Anglia once, but the chap couldn't name the church. It was:

> "Poor Dimity Ann,
>   Her tooken one can
>   Too many, so her vomit,
>   And that done it." '

'Well,' McMaster concluded, 'see you when you've gloated over your Sheila.' He pointed to one of the figures carved on the uprights of the doorway. 'Talking of sheilas,' he said, 'I wish that fellow didn't remind me of Gloria Mundy.'

'*Gloria mundi*, according to the learned professor who tried to teach me Latin,' I said.

'No,' said McMaster, 'I don't mean the glory of the world. I mean a girl I used to date until I found out what a little tramp she was and ditched her. She used to wear a cap like that one, and a sort of ridged and ruckled sweater to try to hide how thin she was. His chain mail reminds me of it. She also used to knot a long silk scarf thing round her waist to keep her pants up because she really hadn't any hips to hang them on to, and the ends of the scarf used to hang down in front in just the way that chap's seem to do.'

'I suppose she carried a sword over her shoulder, too,' I said ironically.

'No,' he replied seriously, 'not a sword, but whenever it was sunny she carried a parasol and used to slant it over her shoulder in just that way. She was partly redheaded, you see, so she burnt to an unbecoming brick-red and then began to peel if she allowed Phoebus Apollo to take any liberties with her complexion. Oh, well, never mind Gloria. Come with me for a drink when you've finished with the church. I'll be somewhere around the grounds. I have a proposition to put to you and I've got a pub in Hereford which I think you'll like.'

'You've got a pub? You're a Mine Host?'

'No. I'm on the board of directors of a chain of hotels and the one in Hereford belongs to our group. We have a number of places which are meant to attract tourists, particularly foreign tourists. We have others for commercial travellers and to accommodate coach parties and bodies attending conferences and the Rotary people and all that sort of thing, but, so far as you are concerned, I am not including these. What we want is an updating of our brochures for our top-class tourist hotels. It's a sort of sub-editing job for you, really. A lot of the information – golf courses, stately homes and castles, old churches and cathedrals, areas of unspoilt natural beauty, facilities for fishing, pony-trekking, access to riding-stables, all that – is already printed in our booklets, but the information is several years out of date. You would have to check all the various items, especially the routes, and make any additions and alterations you thought necessary, bearing in mind that the readers will be on holiday and bent on enjoying themselves in various ways which may or may not be your idea of pleasure.'

'How long is all this supposed to take? I mean, how many hotels are there and where are they situated?'

'There is nothing further north than Yorkshire. We've got a couple there, one in Norfolk, a couple in Worcestershire, one in Suffolk, one in Dorset, two in Devon, two in Cornwall, two in Sussex, one in Kent and this one in Hereford. You can lump some of them together, I should think. Everybody has a car nowadays and a hundred miles means nothing. We can give you until the end of November to send us the stuff so that the printers can get it out for next season. Oh, a photograph for each brochure would be nice. That's a pretty good camera you've got. You will live free at the hotels, get a generous petrol allowance and a certain amount of credit at the hotel bars and, of course, your pay.' He told me what this would be and added, 'I had thought of going up to town this afternoon to ask a newspaper editor I know whether he could put me on to anybody for this job, but I would far rather have you.'

We met again twenty minutes later, when I had examined the rest of the church and he, I suppose, had searched for a headstone to add to his collection. The church was small and, in any case, I was able to purchase two descriptions of it, with some excellent drawings and photographs, when I had been inside the building. Hardie expressed appreciation of the churchyard, but had not been able to add to his gallery of epitaphs.

'Some of these graves are those of children,' he said, 'and that depresses me. Did you get any joy out of your sheila-ma-gig?'

'I couldn't even identify her,' I said. He sighed and then laughed.

'Damned if I'm sure whether I could identify Gloria herself nowadays,' he said, 'and I should class her as the queen of the sheila-ma-gigs.'

'A rather rude lady?' I asked, quoting my own words.

'A damned dangerous one, anyway,' he said. 'If you're ready, let's go.'

The hotel was all that he had claimed for one of his 'specials' and gave me some idea of the kind of work he expected me to do. It was outside the town, had its own golf course of nine holes and the gardens went down in three broad terraces to an immense lawn. Beyond this there was a reed-fringed lake with water-fowl and a smaller pond with water-lilies and goldfish.

The public rooms were high-ceilinged and grand and before lunch he was able to show me a suite of rooms upstairs which the manager told him would not be tenanted until the weekend.

'Kept for visits from royalty or one of the Arab oil-nabobs,' McMaster said. Then he asked me how much time I would need to consider his offer.

'I don't need any time at all,' I replied. 'I'd admire to take it on, as our American cousins used to say.'

'Oh, that's good, Corin. When can you start?' he asked. 'It will take you quite a bit of time, you know, and we must have the stuff by November.'

'I can start as soon as ever you like. Is it all right if I get a book out of my experiences? They should be rather productive of copy.'

'So long as you don't libel us or any of the hotel residents, go ahead, but bear in mind that at these particular hotels we get VIPs and other sensitive plants. Well, what about some lunch? After that, perhaps you'll spare time while I give you a fuller briefing and get you to sign on the dotted line, and all that sort of rot.'

Over lunch he told me more about the girl he had called Gloria. I began it because I asked him whether he was married.

'Lord, yes, for three years now,' he said. 'One reason I had to ditch Gloria was that I'd met Kate. Mind you, I was warned against Gloria by Wotton. You remember Wotton, of course. Front-row forward and capable of even more dirty work in the scrum than most front-row forwards, but a nicer fellow off the field you'd never meet. He had had a brief spell with Gloria himself. Met her on a Mediterranean cruise, I believe. My word, those shipping companies will have something to answer for in the great hereafter! Of course he came to his senses when all the boat-deck-by-moonlight stuff was over and they were back in England, but Gloria, I fancy, was very difficult to dislodge.'

'So he off-loaded her on to you?'

'Not exactly. She picked me up at a night-club. She soon decided I was a better bet than Wotton. This was before he came into the property, of course. She wasn't really the type for either of us. I have never seen a girl so *thin*.'

'What did you have against her, apart from the lack of robustness in her component parts?' I asked. 'Was it because you knew she had had an affair with Wotton?'

'No, I'm broadminded about that sort of thing. It was over. That was all that mattered. I soon found though, that she was dashed expensive. I wouldn't have minded that so much, although she was stretching me to the limits of the salary I was getting in those days, but then I found out that she was double-crossing me with an Italian artist fellow and subsidising him out of my money and by selling the jewellery I'd given her. When I remonstrated with her and we had a row, she had the neck to threaten me with breach of promise if I didn't shut up and continue to play ball. Well, I was pretty sure the case wouldn't succeed, but I knew that, if she brought it, it would queer my pitch with my father, who had promised to take me into partnership; also there was Kate, so I stalled, and then the artist chap committed suicide, poor devil, and there was a fair amount of stink with Gloria mixed up in it. She disappeared out of my life for a time, and I was thankful.'

'Only for a time?'

'Oh, yes. When the suicide became old hat, and things simmered down, she bobbed up again, but by that time I'd got married to Kate. When Gloria knew this, she threatened to write to Kate with details of the night-club pick-up and its aftermath. I told her Kate knew already (although, of course, she didn't) and I said that if Kate received even one dirty letter I would strangle Gloria. I tracked her down and I went so far as to give her a short demonstration of what I would do to her. That really frightened her off. I think she believed I meant what I said, and I reckon I *would* have meant it, too, if she had attempted to muck up my marriage.'

'When we were looking at that church doorway, you told me she was *partly* a redhead. What did you mean by that?'

'Oh, apart from her extreme emaciation – although she ate like a starving wolf when I took her out – she had one very unusual feature.

12

She was auburn-haired on one side of her head and coal-black on the other.'

'Dyed, to create an effect?'

'No. Before I rumbled that she was playing me up, I used to help her wash her hair. The colours were genuine enough. She told me one of her ancestors had been burnt as a witch and that all the female descendants had had half their hair red and the other half black ever since. I could well believe the witchcraft story. The way Gloria could charm the money out of my pockets was witchcraft enough for me. I nearly went to the money sharks, I was so desperate, but came to my senses and made a clean breast of things to the family lawyer. He subbed up on the strength of my expectations – he had drawn up my father's will – and I married Kate.'

'So you haven't heard from Gloria again?'

'No, and, until I saw that fellow carved on that doorway, I've never even thought of her since I threatened to kill her. Not that I now retain any really hard feelings towards her. The Lord who made the little green apples also made the little gold-diggers, I suppose. I'd like to know why the artist chap committed suicide, though. She must have led him the devil of a dance.'

'Artists, like women, are kittle cattle,' I said. 'There's no accounting for them.' We finished lunch, and in the lounge he drafted out a simple form of contract for me to sign and I promised to begin work on the hotel brochures as soon as I had arranged my own affairs. I had booked a room for that night in a hotel at Tewkesbury but, before I went there after I had left him, I decided to pay another visit to Kilpeck church.

The early summer evening was still light enough to allow me to distinguish the figures and carvings on the south door. I stood in front of it and apostrophised the swordbearer in the Phrygian cap.

'Well, Gloria, old fellow, you've done me proud today,' I said. Of course, the evening was drawing in, so I could not see his features all that well, but I could have sworn that, as I spoke, the Celtic warrior winked at me and grinned.

3

Beeches Lawn

It had been agreed that McMaster would send a complete set of brochures to my home address so that I could be armed and well-prepared, so to speak, for my mission. I decided to accept his tip of lumping some of the hotels together, as it was unlikely that tourists who had spent a week or a fortnight in, for instance, Norfolk, would then go and stay in Suffolk, or that those who had stayed at one of his hotels in Yorkshire would then go and spend time and money in the other.

When I had prepared my way by making notes and studying guide-books, the month of May was almost at its end, but careful planning convinced me that, with any luck, I could finish the job by the end of October at the latest. I decided to start with Yorkshire, work southwards to Norfolk, Suffolk, Kent and Sussex, then take in Worcestershire and Herefordshire and finish up with Cornwall, Devon and Dorset.

The whole thing took even less time than I had allowed. Some of the brochures needed little alteration, although I made fresh road-plans where there were alternative or new routes, referring for these to the very latest motoring atlas, and I took great trouble to select and photograph what I thought would be an attractive frontispiece for each little book.

I enjoyed the work, was fairly lucky with the weather and by mid-September I was able to send in most of the amended brochures. The hotels at which I had been staying were all much of a muchness, however, in spite of their comfort and luxury, and, after more than three months of them, I was very pleased to receive an invitation to stay for a week with my old friend Anthony Wotton at his ancestral home in the Cotswolds. As for the red-and-black-haired, skeletal Gloria, I had forgotten all about her.

'I have told Celia about you and she has read one of your novels and is looking forward to meeting you,' wrote Anthony.

He had been a bachelor when I had heard from him last. I assumed (correctly, as it turned out) that Celia was his wife. I could not imagine him married. However, I need have had no qualms on Anthony's behalf. Celia was a charming woman of about his own age and she made me welcome as though she was sincerely pleased to see me.

'I don't know why you haven't been here before,' she said. I explained that I had often visited Anthony at his London flat before old Mr Wotton died and his son inherited the estate, but had never been invited to Beeches Lawn before.

'No, his father and Anthony didn't get on,' she said when she was showing me the room I was to have. 'Anthony thought he might will this place away from him, but he didn't, and I think they were reconciled towards the end. Fortunately' – she smiled – 'the old gentleman took to me and approved of the marriage.'

'He could hardly help it,' I said, looking appreciatively at her. She laughed, told me when to come down for cocktails and left me to unpack, bathe and change. I went to the window, a deep bay which gave good views of the garden and the hills, and looked out. I have always loved the Cotswolds ever since, as a boy, I used to stay with a gamekeeper at Nescomb and learnt country lore from him. He was a wonderful naturalist and could recognise every wild plant that grew. He showed me where the badgers had made their sett under a bank in the woods and where the various birds built their nests. He showed me where there was a fox's den and where to see the now almost extinct red squirrels before those tree-rats, the grey squirrels, took over. He taught me how to shoot, how to recognise every tree in the woods which surrounded his cottage, how to stack wood for the Cotswold winter, how to cook over a wood fire, and how to make cunning flies for fishing by using the feathers of jays. He showed me a green woodpecker, taught me how to handle ferrets and took me to see a grave he revered. It was not in the churchyard, where he himself is buried, but by the side of a woodland ride along which the young owner of the place, before it was sold to become a public school, loved to ride his horse and where he had asked to be laid so that he could dream he was riding there again. The gamekeeper's name was Will Smith and he lived in a stone-built cottage about a mile from the village. I think I liked him better than any man I have ever known.

His father had been a gamekeeper before him. They were not Gloucestershire people, but came from Norfolk, and Will never lost that note at the end of a Norfolk sentence which always seems to ask a question. I was reminded of him when I looked out at the hills. Beeches Lawn was just outside Hilcombury, which is not all that far from Nescomb. I thought, as I looked over to the hills, that I would visit Nescomb again, although I knew that, with Will Smith gone, I could never recapture the old magic of his woods and walks, or that of the long lane which led from the stream and the village street up the hill to his cottage, a lane in which the 'weeds . . . grow long, lovely and lush' and the wild flowers proliferate as they please. There was history, too, in that lane. The big, striped, edible snails introduced by the Roman conquerors were still to be found among the weeds and grasses, and the Chedworth villa was not all that far away, and neither were Cirencester and Gloucester.

Meanwhile, my present surroundings were pleasant and peaceful enough. Below me was an immense sweep of lawn. Among trees which, with some bushes between, divided it into two unequal parts, stood an immense lime tree, the largest I have ever seen, and there was a magnificent copper beech at the other end of the garden. Beyond the further part of the lawn, the ground, I thought, might slope down to a little stream, and beyond this again I could see an occasional vehicle making its way along the road to the town.

At the other end of the lawn there were flowerbeds and on my way up to the house, when I had parked my car, I had passed greenhouses, a flourishing kitchen garden and a mighty apple tree laden with fruit. For some reason I have never been able to explain, although the words turned out to be prophetic, I found myself murmuring, as I looked out upon this peaceful and attractive scene:

> 'And pleasant is the fairy land
> For them that in it dwell,
> But aye at end of seven years,
> They pay a teind to hell.'

'Teind' is a due or a tax, but what, I wondered, had made me think of hell in a place like Beeches Lawn? All I could think of was that the copper beech tree had put the thought of evil into my mind. I would have been about twelve years old, I suppose, when I first came across the Sherlock Holmes stories, and I still think that the twelfth adventure is one of the most spine-tingling tales in the series. That 'prodigiously stout man with a very smiling face and a great heavy chin which rolled down in fold upon fold' has always seemed to me a much more sinister and frightening figure than Colonel Lysander Stark or any other of Conan Doyle's villains.

On the following morning Anthony showed me around. The stables had been converted to garages and the pigsties were empty. I remember he remarked that he was glad to be so near the town as to be virtually part of it, otherwise he might be expected to hunt, 'and all that sort of time-wasting nonsense, old boy. Anyway, I'm a Londoner and, like the film-star ladies, I am happiest among my books,' he said, 'now that I've given up rugger.'

His was a curious property in some ways. Within his boundaries were two other dwellings, and these were not estate cottages, but houses in the full sense of the word. One was a beautiful old place which had been the original family dwelling. I, for one, would never have abandoned it. It was stone-built and charming, a typical Cotswold manor house.

'It's said to be haunted,' he told me, 'but the fact is that it became too small to house my great-great-grandfather's family, so he let it decay. My great-grandfather had it done up and used to keep a woman there. She was supposed to catalogue the library here and help with the household accounts, but rumour, of course, told a different story. My grandfather left the house to rot, but it's not in such a bad state as all that. I think I shall do it up again and let it as a couple of holiday flats. I would only need to put another bathroom in and, I suppose, another kitchen, but I'm considering an offer from somebody who is willing to buy it as it stands. The only problem is the staircase, which is in a parlous state and dangerous.'

We retraced our steps, took the path round the lawn to a field, crossed this and came out into a roughly surfaced lane. I noticed that the field boasted a small pavilion.

'Yes,' he said, when I mentioned this, 'a prep school rent the field from me for games. I charge only a peppercorn rent, of course. I like kids and these are very decent little chaps. I have the headmaster to dinner occasionally, so as to maintain the *entente cordiale*. It works very well. The chap who wants to make me an offer for the old house is this same headmaster. If he comes up with any reasonable figure, I think I shall let him have it. It would save me a lot of trouble and expense as he would do it up to suit himself, because I should sell it as it stands and it would need quite a lot of alteration, I suppose, before I could convert it into flats.'

'It's a charming old place,' I said. 'What is it like inside?'

'Coberley – that's the headmaster – has the only key at present, as I've mislaid mine. I'll get it off him while you're here and show you round.'

'Why does he want to buy it?'

'Goodness knows. I suppose the school is expanding. The kids are mostly day boys, but I believe there are a few boarders.'

'Won't it interfere with your privacy to have youngsters passing your windows on their way to the playing field?'

'They won't need to do that. They will go out by the way you brought your car in and then walk along the road. You can get to the playing field that way, past this next house I'm going to show you.'

This house was a fair way along a lane. It turned out to be a vast, dark, grim-looking place of which the ground-floor windows were barred. Even the front door with its iron-ended bell-pull looked forbidding. It reminded me of the entrance to a gaol.

'It doesn't belong to the estate,' said Anthony. 'We sold it a hundred years ago. A colony of craftsmen have it now, but it used to be a convent for nuns.'

'Poor girls!' I said, looking at the barred windows and the forbidding exterior of the big, dark house.

'Not necessarily, Corin. As Wordsworth put it:

> ' "Nuns fret not at their convent's narrow room,
>   And hermits are contented with their cells,
>   And students with their pensive citadels."

'I think you and I are enough of like mind to agree with him.'

'Perhaps,' I said. 'Anyway, it's peaceful enough here. I thought perhaps I might rough out my next book while I'm with you. You'll be glad for me to be occupied.' He glanced sideways at me, but said nothing and the bombshell burst early on the following day, the Saturday. There was to be a house-party.

The bad news came when Celia opened her letters and came to the last one.

'Well, that's everybody,' she said. 'Karen has accepted at her leisure, the rude little beast. She always does leave everything to the last minute. I suppose she hopes something more exciting than a visit to us will turn up. She wants to bring somebody called William Underedge with her.'

'Who's he?' asked Anthony.

'How should I know? The current boyfriend, I suppose.'

'Where will you put him?'

'On a camp bed in one of the attics. It won't matter where I put him. He'll sleep with Karen anyway, if I know her.'

'He may be a sort of young Sir Galahad. You never know who Karen is going to pick up.'

'If he is, he won't mind the camp bed and bumping his head on the beams in the attic, so that's still all right.'

The guests turned up at intervals during the afternoon and by tea-time everybody was with us. The delinquent Karen turned out to be a fresh-looking up-and-coming young miss, not particularly pretty but engaging enough and possessing a certain amount of spontaneous charm, due, I think, to the fact that she took it for granted that everybody she met was going to like her. In so thinking she was probably right. People are apt to take you at your own self-evaluation.

Her escort, whom she had wished upon her hostess at such short notice, was a stocky, swarthy, gravely earnest young man who turned out to be the son of a local mill-owner. I heard him explaining himself apologetically to Celia.

'If I could have trusted her to drive here without smashing herself up,' he said, 'I wouldn't have pushed in on you, you know. I mean, it seems awful cheek when you don't even know me.'

'We soon shall put that right,' said Celia kindly, 'and we are very pleased you could come. Have you known Karen long?'

'Oh, on and off, you know; just on and off. I mean, everybody goes round with a gang these days, don't they, and she and I are in the same crowd. We sing Bach and five of us play chamber music.'

'Not – surely not Karen?'

'Oh, I weaned her off the disco stuff long ago and now she sings Bach and I'm hoping to get her to take lessons on the cello. She's got the figure for the cello, I think, although, of course, she'll never look quite like Suggia, I'm afraid.'

I realised that Celia, whose niece Karen was, was looking at the earnest young man with something not far short of awe, and it occurred to me that William Underedge was an incarnation of one of the great fictional creations of the Master of English Prose. I put it to Celia later.

'The Efficient Baxter personified, wouldn't you say?'

'Good heavens, no, Corin! I think William Underedge is perfectly sweet.'

'Not even efficient?'

'I just hope he's efficient enough to make Karen marry him. He would be very good for her, I think. By the way, don't let my aunt back you into a corner and talk to you about the *Malleus Maleficarum*. She will, if she gets half a chance.'

There were two extraordinary old ladies in the party. Both had come unescorted and both, I suspected, were quite notably eccentric. This

aunt, who was really Celia's great-aunt, was tall and of intimidating
bulk. She wore pince-nez with two gold chains which looped over her
ears and dangled safely on to her immense bosom when she discarded
the glasses. She spoke in almost a whisper unless she became excited,
but then her voice screamed like a particularly indignant seagull or
boomed like a bittern heard through an amplifier. This happened
chiefly when she was talking on her favourite topic which, as Celia had
warned me, was the *Malleus Maleficarum* of the Dominican priors
Heinrich Kramer and James Sprenger, published in the witchhunting
days of 1486 AD.

'Germans, of course,' Aunt Eglantine belted out across the dinner-
table, 'but, when it comes to sheer thoroughness, there is nobody to
beat them.'

Nobody attempted to contest this. I think all shared my hope that,
so long as she was permitted to proceed unchecked, in the end she
would gallop herself to a standstill. The policy succeeded after a
fashion when she had issued what proved to be a final challenge, but it
succeeded only with the help of Dame Beatrice, our other old lady.

'What's more,' went on Miss Eglantine Brockworth, warming to
her theme, 'it is high time that somebody wrote another *Malleus*.
Witchcraft is rife in the world of today. The powers of evil gather
strength. Even this house is not free from them. Incubi and succubi
are all around us and soon they will be in our midst. They have the
power to destroy us.'

'But no operation of witchcraft can have a permanent effect, according to the authorities you have been quoting,' said Dame Beatrice
Lestrange Bradley. 'I believe the reverend fathers went on to say that a
belief that the devil has power to do human bodies any permanent
harm does not appear to conform to the teachings of the Church.'

At mention of the Church, everybody gave great attention to the
food, and there was the slightly uneasy silence which usually follows
the introduction of such a gaffe as to make a reference to religion at any
social gathering. That this interval of silence had been brought about
deliberately by the reptilian old lady opposite me was manifest the
next moment. She looked up, caught my eye, and the ghost of a grin

appeared for a fleeting instant on her yellow countenance. At that moment I fell in love with Dame Beatrice Lestrange Bradley.

Celia, as a good hostess, started conversation off again by introducing some innocuous topic – I forget what it was – and we all relaxed. Fortunately Aunt Eglantine ('my name comes not from Shakespeare, but from Chaucer') elected to retire early, so we were quit of her and the *Malleus Maleficarum* for the rest of the evening.

Then there were the other guests. The first two who had arrived were the Coberleys. Cranford Coberley was headmaster of the school which rented Anthony's field, who might also be considering the purchase of the old house, so I took it that the occasional dinner to which my host had referred had developed, this time, into a weekend stay. As the school was so close at hand, I suppose Coberley thought that he could pop back at any moment if an emergency presented itself or an anxious mum turned up to enquire after the health and happiness of little Johnny, as the staff knew where to contact the headmaster. He struck me as a taciturn, colourless man, but perhaps he was more dynamic when he was in harness. From what I know of small boys, he would need to be.

To my mild astonishment, it appeared that he had yoked himself (her second marriage, I learnt later) to a ravishing beauty. Marigold Coberley, slimmer than the Venus of Milo, more golden than Helen of Troy, was the loveliest girl I had ever seen or ever expect to see. It is not possible for me to describe her, except to say, with Yeats, 'Oh, that I were young again, and held her in my arms!'

As a matter of fact, I was very much younger than Coberley, but let the quotation stand for what it is worth, namely, 'the desire of the moth for the star; of the night for the morrow'. My desire for Marigold Coberley was not more lustful than that, but, in any case, I would have shared Yeats's despairing cry, even though my age, as such, was not against me. Besides, beauty such as hers is intimidating and, to me, sacrosanct. I was content to be the courtier in the palace, not a man who thought he had a claim to the throne.

The other two were an engaged couple and seemed pleasant enough young people, although I had the impression that Roland Thornbury, who was vaguely related to Anthony and had expectations from him if Celia had no children, might turn into a domestic tyrant once he was married to the self-effacing Kay Shortwood. I put this opinion to Celia and Anthony after everybody else had gone to bed. Celia gave a short, expressive, derisive laugh.

'Don't you believe it, Corin,' she said. 'Roland is safely hooked and she'll play him with guile until she's got him just where she wants him. After that, it will be the landing-net and the gaff, and goodbye to Roland except as a meal-ticket. She knows very well that at present Roland is Anthony's heir. However, I am quite young enough to have children. I don't particularly want them, but it would be rather fun to see Kay Shortwood's reactions if she knew there was Roland's supplanter on the way.'

'I had no idea you could be so vindictive,' I said, laughing.

'Oh, there's a bitch in every woman,' she responded, 'and I particularly dislike that mealy-mouthed little gold-digger. However, Roland always wants to bring her with him and they are engaged to be married, so what can we do?'

'As we appear to be doing, which is to leave Roland to his fate and to the minding of his own business,' said Anthony.

'A Daniel come to judgment!' she quoted ironically. 'What do you make of Dame Beatrice, Corin?'

'I rather wondered why she was here. You two – I speak mostly for Anthony – have never mentioned that you were acquainted with her, yet I understand that she's a celebrity in her own line.'

'She got me out of an awful mess in the south of France once. That was before Celia and I were married,' said Anthony. 'I was accused of murdering a little girl and Dame Beatrice got the case stopped and told the police who the murderer was. I don't know how she did it, but she did it all right.'

'Possibly by "the monstrous power of witchcraft",' I suggested, 'or so Celia's aunt might say.'

'Talking of witches,' said Celia, with a chuckle, 'wasn't it clever of Dame Beatrice to match herself against Aunt Eglantine and win?'

'Anybody could do it, I suppose, provided they had read the *Malleus* and remembered what they'd read,' said Anthony.

'I tried reading it once,' said Celia, 'if only to be able to keep up sides with Aunt. However, in Montague Summers's translation from the Latin there are five hundred and sixty-five closely printed pages, so I didn't stay the course.'

'That's your aunt's strong suit, of course,' said Anthony. 'She trades on the fact that nobody she is acquainted with has read the stuff, so that she can pontificate away to her heart's content without fear of being challenged. Now that she has come up against somebody who knows the text even better than she does, I expect we shall have a bit of peace until Dame Beatrice goes. Unfortunately she's got to attend a conference in Cheltenham, so she'll be leaving us before lunch tomorrow.'

'I could wish to be better acquainted with her,' I said.

'I'm not so sure you're wise, old boy,' said Anthony. 'She's consultant psychiatrist to the Home Office and has probably already got you sized up as a lad who can bear watching.'

'The girl who *can* bear watching, although not in the insulting sense your reference to me suggests, is Mrs Coberley,' I said indiscreetly. Anthony chipped in at once, and I knew he was not joking.

'You keep your eyes to yourself, or there'll be murder done,' he said. 'Coberley ain't as quiet as he looks; and he's as possessive as the devil where his lily-and-rose is concerned.'

4
Unbidden Guest

I woke early next day and went to the window to see the long shadow of the copper beech lying slantwise across the lawn in the morning sun. Nobody else was stirring when I went downstairs except a house-maid busy in the dining-room. She asked whether I would like my breakfast, but I replied that I would wait until the usual hour, when-ever that was.

'The mistress has hers on a tray, sir, and Sandra mostly puts out the dining-room sideboard at nine, sir.'

I decided to take my car for a short run. It would disturb nobody, as it was parked at a considerable distance from the house. As I walked past the flowerbeds and through the kitchen garden to get to it, I felt an urge to look again at the family's other house, that which had once been the lodging of Anthony's great-grandfather's mistress. Just as I reached it I met Coberley coming from the opposite direction. We exchanged greetings.

'I wondered whether it was possible to go inside,' I said, indicating the house.

'Oh, I've got a key,' he said. 'I've got an option on the place. It would make a storehouse for all the junk my little boys collect. Dear me, what rubbish they do bring in, but children are inveterate collec-tors. The dangerous objects are already in a wooden box in the old house. I intend to start – '

'A school museum?' I suggested.

'Call it what you like. I've offered to buy the house from Wotton and do it up. By the time the parents have paid for it I shall see that there will be enough money left over to enlarge the pavilion in Wotton's field.'

'High finance,' I commented.

'Oh, one thing works in with another, and I do well with Common Entrance, so the parents are pleased.' He produced a key and opened the front door. 'I wouldn't try the stairs,' he said. 'You could break your neck on them.'

'So they wouldn't be safe for Great-aunt Eglantine,' I said lightly.

'That old monstrosity will bring trouble on herself if she insists on regaling us with extracts from the Hammer of Evil,' he said seriously. 'She doesn't know what she's talking about. Those two Dominicans who wrote the *Malleus* were fair, just and merciful men, considering the times in which they lived. They were also great ecclesiastical lawyers and, I would say, haters of heresy but not of heretics. They genuinely desired to save souls from perdition and only to condemn bodies to those ghastly punishments when everything else had been tried. But that overweight dabbler in the occult is treading on danger-ous ground because she is only out for sensationalism and, once you get that bug, you can land up almost anywhere. Those men quite rightly saw witchcraft as the supreme heresy and not only as a reli-gious but as a political danger. She has neither their intellect nor their concern for the human race, but only for her own entertainment and the assertion of her ego. I'm told that in her youth she learnt to toss the caber. No, I don't believe it, either,' he said in response to my ejacu-lation, 'but I believe that in her day she was a first-class tennis player. I suppose all the muscle has gone to adipose tissue and that she's taken up this witchcraft stuff to compensate her for losing the plaudits of the crowd.'

'But there's nothing in witchcraft,' I said.

'Not if you don't believe in it. All the same, I've seen some very strange things in my time. What do you think of the only picture in the place?' He led the way to a ground-floor room at the back of the house. 'It belongs to Wotton, of course, but, in any case, I should dis-card it before I took over the house. It is not an object on which I should desire young boys to speculate.'

The picture hung on a wall opposite the window, so that the light of the emerging day fell full on it. It was the portrait (I guessed that it was a portrait) of a naked girl. She was thin to the point of emaciation, and yet the artist had contrived to give her a sensuousness, almost a voluptuousness, which seemed quite at variance with her meagre, childish body, long thin legs and unformed, skinny arms.

There was nothing in the face, either, of any pretensions to beauty. She was snub-nosed and her eyes were set close together. She had a low forehead and the most striking thing about her was her hair. It fell only to her shoulders, but was of two unimaginably contrasting colours, violently red on the right side of her head, almost coal-black on the other. In one apparently nerveless hand she held a rose between her thumb and first finger. The other hand fell lifelessly down to reach her thigh.

'Well?' said Coberley, watching me.

'She is a witch,' I said, 'and the artist was a genius.'

We strolled back to Wotton's house. I had forgotten my plan to take out my car. I wondered when the portrait had been painted, and whether Celia had ever seen it.

Aunt Eglantine did not appear at breakfast, but everyone else except Celia was there. Dame Beatrice, who took nothing but toast and coffee, sat next to me and proved to have read my biography of Horace Walpole.

'He was a visitor to a property a few miles from here,' she said, 'and recommended it to a friend of his, William Cole. Have you been to Prinknash Abbey?'

'No. My book concerned itself mostly with his writings after he retired to Strawberry Hill.'

'You would enjoy Prinknash. The Benedictines have it now, and have built a new and much enlarged abbey. The old building is used as a retreat house, so you can probably get permission to be shown over it, if you are interested. It is a lovely Early Tudor building and the west court is particularly fine. On the outer wall of the east court there is a bas-relief of a young man reputed to be Henry the Eighth.'

'I shouldn't think that would find much favour with the monks,' I said lightly.

'Oh, the thing would have been sculptured long before the Dissolution. There are connections with Catherine of Aragon. Her badge of a pomegranate surmounted by a crown is to be seen here and there, and on the ceiling of the old chapel, which dates back to the later Middle Ages and has a misericord to every stall, there is the badge of Edward the Fourth, a rose and a falcon.'

At this point a servant came in to say that I was wanted on the telephone. As the only person to whom I had given my address in case there should be any queries about the brochures was McMaster, I guessed correctly that the call must come from him. I took it and went sadly back to the dining-room to tell Wotton that I had to leave forthwith.

'I promised to place myself at McMaster's disposal,' I said apologetically, 'so I'm afraid I shall have to go and see him.'

'Oh, but why? Couldn't you suggest meeting him here? I would like to see the old buster again. We used to play in the college fifteen, if you remember. Do ask him to come. Is he married?'

'Yes, to somebody called Kate,' I replied.

'Well, tell him to bring the girl along. We have plenty of room now that Dame Beatrice has to leave us.'

I had discovered that Celia had repented of putting the earnest young Underedge on a camp bed in one of the attics. (In fact, I doubted whether that had ever been her serious intention.) 'Roland and Kay are leaving after lunch, too.' Anthony added.

Except for Wotton himself, the dining-room was empty when I came back from the telephone for the second time.

'Grateful thanks from McMaster,' I said. 'Kate's decided not to come. He hates leaving her, but won't be here long. He thinks he and I can be through in about an hour.'

'Oh, good. It would have been a great pity to lose you so soon after your arrival,' said Anthony.

'Thanks very much.'

'You've made a big hit with Celia. She has never met a real live author before. I noticed you seemed to be getting on extremely well with Dame Beatrice, too. A pity you had to say goodbye to her so soon.'

'She was telling me I ought to visit Prinknash Abbey.'

'Oh, yes, you must do that. Apart from a lovely old house which used to be the monastery before they needed more room, the setting is quite supremely beautiful. The place lies in a valley surrounded by wooded hills. You can't imagine a more delightful spot. I'm glad Dame Beatrice mentioned it.'

'Does one ask any sort of permission to go and see the place?'

'Oh, no. The grounds are open to the public. I don't know whether you could be shown over the house, but at least you could look at the outside of it. It really is a picture.'

'Talking of pictures,' I said, 'Coberley showed me the one in your other house.'

'That's the lady my great-grandfather kept there,' he said. 'She was reputed to have been a witch. I don't have the picture in this house because it's supposed to be unlucky. I'd get rid of it if it weren't such a marvellous bit of painting.'

'Strangely enough, McMaster described it to me,' I said.

'McMaster? He couldn't have done. He's never seen it. Of course, though! You mean he described Gloria Mundy to you.'

I could feel that there was tension in the air, so, to relieve it, this time it was I who changed the subject. I asked a question which it would have been impossible to put in the presence of the old lady herself.

'You told me how you came to be acquainted with Dame Beatrice, but what was she doing here? I shouldn't have thought psychiatry was much in your line. Was she here on the same terms as the rest of us, merely as a guest?'

'It was Celia's idea. She thinks – and with some justification – that poor old Aunt Eglantine is going off her rocker, so Dame Beatrice came to take a look at her and to advise us whether treatment is necessary.'

'How is Aunt Eglantine going to respond, if Dame Beatrice does think it's necessary?'

'I don't know what the outcome will be. Dame Beatrice will send us a report.'

McMaster was to join us after lunch, so, accepting Wotton's offer to put a writing-desk in my room, I watched the four young people go off for a Sunday morning drive in Roland Thornbury's car and then went upstairs to go through my notes for McMaster's brochures so that I should be prepared for his arrival.

The desk Wotton had given me faced the window, so that every time I looked up I had a view of the lawn, the trees and the hills. There was not a great deal to go through in my notes, and at about eleven a servant came in with coffee, a flask of whisky and some biscuits. I had disposed of the coffee and biscuits, and was relaxing and wondering what queries McMaster might have to put to me concerning the brochures, when I saw a girl approaching the house. She was dressed in jeans and a sweater and was carrying a small suitcase. She was a stranger to me until I realised that I had seen, not herself, but a portrait of her. Allowing for the fact that she was clad, whereas the picture I had seen was that of a nude, she bore an uncanny resemblance to the picture of the girl in the old house. What clinched it was her hair. As she approached my window she had pulled off the woollen cap she was wearing and her hair, which had been tucked up under it, fell to her shoulders. Half of it was a fiery red, the rest of it was black.

She passed in front of my window, but very shortly she was back again. I was standing up by this time and she must have seen me, for she called out, 'Hi, there! Come and let me in.'

The window was open at the top. I pushed it up from the bottom and leant out.

'Ring the bell,' I advised her. 'I can't let you in. I'm a visitor here.'

'This is Tony's pad, isn't it?'

'It belongs to Mr Wotton.'

'Well, that's Tony. I'm his cousin Gloria.'

'The front door is round the corner. You must have passed it just now,' I told her. She made a very rude gesture, walked on, and I heard the doorbell ring.

The four young ones had returned from their drive. Aunt Eglantine, who had taken affectionate leave of Dame Beatrice, was looking smug. Dame Beatrice, with the expression of a satisfied snake, had been escorted to her car, Celia, at the foot of the table, was looking pensive, Anthony, at its head, appeared gloomy and the newcomer, seated opposite Aunt Eglantine, was glancing brightly round at the company.

Anthony had introduced her to us as Miss Gloria Mundy, but made no mention of relationship. When it was my turn to greet her I had said that coincidence was a very strange thing.

'Another friend of mine knows you,' I said, 'a man named McMaster. He mentioned you only a few weeks ago.'

'Oh, dear old Hardie,' she said. 'We had great times together. He was tremendous fun.'

'He's coming here after lunch,' said Celia. 'You'll be able to talk over old times, as perhaps you had hoped to do with Anthony.'

'He is coming on business,' said Anthony. 'The person he will want to talk to is Corin.'

'He will want to talk to me,' said Gloria. She continued to look brightly but, I thought, challengingly around her at the others seated at table. Soup had been served, and she sat there opposite Aunt Eglantine, her soup spoon poised. She waved it. 'What a bevy of beauties you have assembled, Tony darling,' she said, looking straight at Marigold Coberley, 'I wonder how you dare collect young, pretty girls around you now you are a married man. It was different in the old days, wasn't it? My word! You stepped high and handsome then, you sporty boy, didn't you? Don't tell me the old Adam is coming out again.'

It was Aunt Eglantine who made what I thought was the adequate response to this. She picked up a flat, soft bread-roll and lobbed it neatly and accurately into Gloria's well-filled plate of soup.

'Well, her ancient skills have not deserted her,' said Celia, referring to the incident. 'Appalling though it was of Aunt, and providing as it did visible proof that we had good reason for having Dame Beatrice take a look at her, it nearly killed me not to laugh.'

'Dame Beatrice would have remained unmoved,' I said.

'I expect she is accustomed to eccentric patients. I thought Cranford

Coberley looked distressed. I expect he was glad none of his boys was present to have such a bad example set them.' Celia seemed to hesitate for a moment and then, presumably because there was no one in the room except ourselves – for McMaster had arrived and Anthony was showing him over the estate before Hardie and I settled down with the brochures – out she came with it.

'Corin! That awful girl! Whatever could Anthony have seen in her? And why on earth should she come here? He finished with her years ago.'

'Oh, I expect she found herself in the neighbourhood and thought she would look the two of you up.'

Celia was not pleased. She asked angrily, 'Oh, why do men always try to cover up for one another?'

'To oppose the monstrous regiment of women. Besides, aren't women – don't women – do the same?' I asked.

'Sometimes, I suppose, sometimes not. Well, I'm not always grateful to Aunt Eglantine, but I'm thankful to her for finding a way of getting rid of Gloria Mundy.'

'Yes, the soup did splash about a bit, didn't it? I wonder why there is always three times as much liquid when it's spilt than when it is in the bowl.'

'One of Parkinson's Laws, isn't it? I'll tell you one thing, Corin. That girl is up to mischief of some sort.'

'What sort?'

'If I knew that, I'd know what to do about it. I wish Marigold Coberley hadn't laughed when the soup went all over Gloria. Did you see the look she got while we were all mopping Gloria up?'

'I wonder why that staggeringly beautiful young woman married a stick-in-the-mud like Coberley?'

'Thereby hangs a tale, but it's not my story. You must ask Anthony.'

Anthony, coming into the room, said firmly, 'As I tried to tell you, he's a ravening lion where she's concerned. He risked a lot to marry her, you know. She stood trial for killing her former husband and only got off by the skin of her teeth. Surely you remember the case, Corin?

Her name then was Maria Pinzón Campville. Coberley was called as a prosecution witness (most unwillingly, of course) and he married her as soon as the case was over. He threw up a lucrative job and bought the school just to get her away from all the publicity. He told me the story last Christmas when I'd got him nicely sozzled, but it's old hat now.'

'And *did* she do it?' I asked. 'Kill her husband, I mean?'

'*Quíen sabe?* There were nine men on the jury, and you know how beautiful she is.'

'At least one of the three women must have voted for an acquittal, though,' I said, 'and probably carried the other two with her. There are always women who think a man deserves everything he gets, so perhaps these ladies of the jury approved of the murder. The war between the sexes waxes fiercely in these days of women's emancipation and the competition for top jobs, I suppose.'

'I've got a bone to pick with you,' said Hara-kiri after we had gone through my notes and alterations.

'With me? But you said you liked what I'd done with the brochures.'

'I'm not talking about the brochures. Do you remember my mentioning Gloria Mundy when we last met?'

'Yes, of course I remember.'

'And I gave you an impression of what I thought of her?'

'Unfavourable, on the whole, as I remember it.'

'Well, I think you might have told me she was staying in the house when you relayed old Anthony's invitation.'

'But she isn't staying here. She breezed in all unexpectedly and had to be asked to stay for lunch. You were probably on your way here by the time she turned up, so I couldn't have let you know, even if I had thought of it. Anyway, there is no question of her staying here. She didn't even stay long enough to finish her lunch. One of the other guests splashed soup all over her, so she upped and went.'

'I spotted her in the kitchen garden after I had left my car.'

'Well, she won't be coming back, that's for sure.'

'You never know. I hope you're right, that's all. How long are *you* staying here?'

'Only until Thursday. Don't worry. I shall be on to the rest of the brochures in just a day or so.'

'That is not what I meant. How did Wotton react when Gloria showed up?'

'I wasn't present at their meeting. I was up here.'

'I wonder what she was after?'

'Wanted a free lunch, perhaps,' I said. 'I don't think she looks any more robust than when you knew her. Did you see her again while you were in the grounds with Wotton?'

'No. She can't have been up to any good coming here, Corin. Was there a hint of Auld Lang Syne, would you say?'

'Honestly, Hardie, I have no idea.'

'Up to no good at all,' he said thoughtfully. 'As for me, I'm going to sprinkle salt all round my bed tonight.'

'Don't tell me you're as superstitious as that!' I said.

He scowled at me, 'That damn girl spells trouble. You mark my words,' he muttered angrily. 'I cut and ran as soon as I spotted that red and black hair above the bushes. I only saw the top of her head, but nobody can mistake her.'

5
Chapter of Accidents

I had no idea what time it was when Roland and Kay left the house. McMaster and I were still upstairs, working on the brochures. The front door was round a corner and so out of sight of my window, but, in any case, I had no time to look out of it. McMaster had wanted one or two additions to the brochures and there was enough to do to keep us busy until almost teatime.

It had been getting darker all the afternoon, so, by the time we went downstairs, I had had the electric light on for the past hour. The full force of the storm struck the house just as we reached the hall.

We heard afterwards that it was the worst storm for ten years. The sky blackened, the windows rattled, doors thought to be shut flew open, the wind shrieked and tore at the trees and bushes, and then the rain came down and deluged the paths and the lawn.

I have never experienced such rain. It blotted out everything as though the house were surrounded by thick fog. The others all fled to their rooms to make certain that the windows were closed, while Anthony, Celia and the servants made the rest of the rounds. A sky-light which had been left open was allowing a spate of water to cascade down the back stairs and for more than five minutes it resisted all attempts to close it.

The cook reported that water was coming in under the back door and part of the guttering gave up the struggle, so that water fell in fountains down one of the outside walls.

'You shouldn't have let that witch-girl in,' pronounced Aunt Eglantine, during the first lull in the storm before its devils' chorus broke out again. 'She's doing all this.'

'You shouldn't have chucked your bread into her soup,' said William Underedge severely. 'I'm afraid you are a very naughty old lady.'

'Karen laughed when I did it.'

'No, I didn't,' said Karen. 'I wouldn't have thought of laughing. I detest hearty humour. It was Mrs Coberley who laughed.'

'People laugh from shock mostly,' said McMaster. 'Isn't that so?'

Before anybody could answer, the doorbell pealed and pealed.

'That's witchcraft, too,' said Aunt Eglantine. 'They always do that when they want to annoy people.'

A maidservant, her cap askew and her shoes soaking wet, announced the return of Kay and Roland. They had decided to take to the byroads, had come to a watersplash which the rain had swollen into a torrent and got their car waterlogged in mid-stream. To complete the disaster, the wind had flung a big branch at them and it had smashed the windscreen.

'We had to abandon the car and get to a garage,' said Roland. 'They won't touch the job until the water ebbs away, so we hired from them and they brought us back. We're soaking.'

As this hardly needed saying, Celia sent them off to get a hot bath and she and Anthony lent them clothes, as all their luggage had been left in the boot of their car.

'I'm very grateful for your offer of a bed for the night,' said McMaster, when the two drowned rats had gone upstairs, 'but I think I ought to be off as soon as the storm gives over.'

'Oh, why?' asked Celia.

'Because you've offered me Miss Shortwood's room, and now she'll be needing it herself.'

'That's all right. Kay could have shared with Karen just for one night, but Dame Beatrice has gone, so her room is available. Do stay. But, anyway, it would have been quite easy.'

Kay came downstairs again before Roland reappeared. Over tea, at which the Coberleys were not present as they had been called back to the school before the storm broke, she asked casually, 'I thought, didn't I, that Miss Mundy had left? Didn't she go after the soup incident at lunch? She *said* she was going, I thought.'

'Oh, she did go,' said Celia, without glancing at Aunt Eglantine, who was wiping buttery fingers down the front of a black velvet gown. 'Yes, she went off in a white-hot rage and I didn't suggest she should stay.'

'Witches are gate-crashers,' said Aunt Eglantine. 'Nobody wants them. They just invite themselves.'

'What do you mean about Gloria?' said Anthony to Kay. 'Of course she went, and no wonder.'

'Then I think you may take it that she has come back,' said Roland, who had just entered the room. 'Tea? Oh, I say, jolly good!' He seated himself. 'She's in the old house. We saw her at the window.'

'But she couldn't get in. Coberley has the only key,' said Anthony.

'Witches can get in anywhere,' said Aunt Eglantine.

'Well, she can't sleep there. There is no bed and no heating,' said Celia. 'As soon as the rain eases off, somebody had better go and bring her back here. I shall have to find somewhere to bed her down, that's all.'

'No. I shall take her to a hotel,' said Anthony. 'She is not going to make a nuisance of herself here.'

'You'll do nothing of the sort,' said McMaster. 'Kate will expect me. I am very grateful, as I said, for your offer of a bed for tonight but, as the weather already seems to be easing off, there is no reason why you should put me up. I'll be the one to go.'

'To make room for Gloria? Perish the thought!' said Anthony.

'No, really, you mustn't go,' said Celia. 'Anthony can telephone the hotel and a taxi can take the wretched woman there. They know us. We often go there on Saturday evenings to dine and dance. They will take her in and Anthony can settle the bill later. It's worth it to make sure that she doesn't come back here. You ring up your wife and tell her you're staying, and then after dinner we'll all settle down and have a cosy time. I'm sure you three old college friends will like to get together and talk over old times in Anthony's den, and I expect the rest of us can amuse ourselves without you. The rain may ease off, but there is bound to be flooding. We don't want you bogged down like Roland and Kay.'

'They should have stuck to the main roads, of course,' said William Underedge.

'Thanks for the hindsight,' said Roland Thornbury angrily.

'Now, now!' said Karen. 'Boys must not be boys in mixed company.' The maid came in to clear away the tea things, and the various parties dispersed to their rooms except for Anthony and Celia. As I, the last to leave, was passing through the doorway into the hall, I heard him say, 'The storm has upset people. Well, I had better see about Gloria, I suppose.'

'I'm sure Roland and Kay are mistaken,' I said, turning round. 'Coberley let me into the old house this morning. She couldn't possibly have got in without the key.'

'Then I had better ring up the school and find out whether Coberley lent it to her,' said Anthony. 'It was not right of him if he did. The house is not yet his property.'

'Do you mind that he took me in there this morning?'

'My dear chap, of course not. It is one thing for him to take somebody in with him; quite another for him to lend the key to somebody else, particularly to somebody who turned up out of the blue and wished herself on us the way Gloria did.'

'I thought you might have been glad to see her,' said Celia. 'She must have been pretty sure of her welcome to have chanced her arm like that.'

'What do you mean? I hate the sight of her.'

I closed the door behind me and left them to it. At the top of the stairs I met McMaster with a towel over his arm.

'Thank God for what Rupert Brooke called "the benison of hot water",' he said. 'What's happening about our precious Gloria? I hope those two made a mistake and she isn't still on the premises.'

'Anthony is going over to find out.' I was tempted to tell him that Gloria, however involuntarily, had already managed to create friction between husband and wife, but I thought better of it. It was no business of mine, anyway.

* * *

When I went downstairs again, I realised that outwardly Anthony and Celia had patched up their differences. Aunt Eglantine had opted for a tray in her room instead of joining us at table, so the company was depleted in numbers, for the Coberleys had decided to remain at the school.

Anthony had been over to the old house and reported that one of the back windows was smashed and that the portrait which Coberley had shown me had disappeared. He supposed that Gloria had broken in and stolen it. He added, without looking at Celia, that he was not sorry it had gone. Gloria had gone, too. However doubtful Anthony had been about the information which Roland and Kay had given him, the disappearance of the picture, together with the broken window (a feature Coberley would have noticed and commented upon when he had shown me over the house) bore out what Roland had said.

Anthony had hammered on the front door, received no answer, and had then gone round to the back and knocked and shouted. There had been no response, so he had climbed in and found the place empty and the picture gone. This he confided only to Celia and myself while we were having cocktails before dinner.

When dinner was over, the four young people played Scrabble for a bit, but soon drifted off to bed. Aunt Eglantine, who had come down after dinner and had been communing either with herself or with the spirits of Kramer and Sprenger, also gave us little of her company. Celia went off to the ground-floor room she had allocated to her own use, and Anthony, McMaster and I settled down in Anthony's den on the first floor and, with the assistance of his whisky, relived our youth by adopting Celia's suggestion and talking over old times.

We broke up at well past midnight. Mopping-up operations seemed to have been completed and the house, except for a faint sound of water dripping from a leaky guttering somewhere, was almost eerily silent.

Breakfast was a silent meal, too. Anthony seemed preoccupied and Celia, who had come downstairs, poured coffee in an absentminded manner. I deduced that their little set-to about Gloria had been resumed, but there had been no sign of any rift at dinner on the previous night. There were no morning papers and when Anthony rang up he was told that the floods had held up deliveries.

Kay came down to say that Roland had a heavy cold. She had been to his room and found him flushed and very irritable. A tray was sent up to him and Celia suggested that somebody had better take his temperature, but Kay said that this was unnecessary, as he was always one to make a fuss if he had so much as a finger-ache. They were going home, anyway, as soon as the garage could bring round Roland's car, she added. Celia, however, armed herself with a thermometer, but she came downstairs to report that Roland's temperature was not much above normal. He had eaten his breakfast, would be down for lunch, and he and Kay would leave directly the car came. Hara-kiri had already departed.

Anthony rang up Coberley and he and Marigold came over. He denied having lent Gloria the key to the old house and, in view of the broken window, there was no reason to disbelieve him.

'I was intrigued to notice the quite uncanny resemblance Miss Mundy's hair and features bore to those of the girl in the picture,' he said, 'and from what I was able to observe of the young lady herself during the short time she was with us – '

'Yes, she is hardly a model who would have been chosen by Sir Peter Paul Rubens, to name but one painter who liked his ladies well-covered,' said Marigold. 'And now be quiet. To my mind, the picture was obscene, and I am glad the little boys are not to see it.'

'The *Malleus Maleficarum* lays down,' said Aunt Eglantine, who was with us at table again, 'that the soul can sometimes effect a change in its own body. That herring-gutted little witch is a case in point. What were you saying about Rubens?'

'Nothing, Aunt dear,' said Celia. 'Marigold was only referring to a portrait in the old house, and that is certainly not a Rubens.'

'He used his wives as his models, they say. He must have fed them well. *They* were not witches,' said Eglantine.

'We were not talking about Rubens, Auntie dear.'

'Yes, you were. I heard you. That girl who is too beautiful for her own good mentioned him.'

Marigold laughed and Anthony said, 'She was only making a comparison.'

'She interrupted her husband's description of the witch, so what she said about Rubens must be important to her.'

Everybody abandoned the argument.

Roland and Kay went off in the early afternoon, the Coberleys returned to the school, and, with everybody gone, the house was left to Anthony, Celia, Aunt Eglantine and myself, for William Underedge had insisted on removing himself and the astonishingly quiescent Karen as soon as Roland and Kay had been seen off.

At breakfast on the following morning Anthony and I did not miss Celia and Aunt Eglantine, for both had decided to breakfast upstairs. Celia came down at ten, but, when half-past eleven struck and there was still no sign of her aunt, enquiries were made.

Aunt Eglantine, it appeared, had gone into the kitchen for toast and coffee instead of waiting for her tray, and had carried these up to her room by way of the back stairs and a little later had passed in front of the kitchen window on her way towards the kitchen garden.

'The silly old thing has gone into the town to shop on her own,' said a worried Celia, 'and she's hopeless at crossing the road.'

'She won't need to cross it if she uses the bridge and only goes to the shopping centre,' said Anthony.

'But it's so naughty of her. I promised I would take her in the car.'

'Not to worry. She'll be all right. After all, I expect that when she's at home she goes shopping by herself. She's reached her seventies without getting herself either arrested or run over, so why should any harm come to her now?'

'Because she's supposed to be in our care. If anything happened to her, we'd be held responsible. I wish you would go out in the car and bring her back.'

'Good Lord, she's not a small child who has strayed away! She may be a little bit eccentric, but she isn't a loony.'

'She's promised to attend Dame Beatrice's London clinic.'

'Only because she likes feeling important. Dame Beatrice told us there is nothing wrong with her except this ridiculous obsession with witchcraft, and that can be dealt with, it seems, if she wants to rid herself of it.'

'If she were *your* aunt – '

'Well, she isn't, thank heaven!'

'Of course you hate her because she saw through that beastly little ex-girlfriend of yours!' Celia flung this at him in a tone I had never thought she could use, then she turned to dash out of the room and ran straight into me.

'Whoops-a-daisy!' I said, fielding her.

'Oh, Corin! You have been listening!' she exclaimed angrily.

'No, but, like the woodcutter in *Make-Believe*, I couldn't help hearing,' I explained.

'Well, don't you agree with me?'

'I always agree with the woman I'm talking to. It saves wear and tear on the nervous system.' Suddenly I thought of Imogen, who had said to me that marriage was not for writers.

'Well, then! Don't you think my aunt may be in danger? She isn't used to traffic,' Celia went on.

'All right, I'll go, if Anthony's busy. I want to go into the town, anyway,' I said.

'Make sure Aunt Eglantine doesn't come back with a baby elephant or a steam-roller,' said Anthony. 'I haven't house-room for those sort of things. Never did have, even in the good old days.'

'No, only for that red-black flame of yours!' said Celia. 'The good old days indeed!'

'It was you who asked the blasted girl to stay to lunch!' He strode up to where we were standing. Celia had extricated herself from my involuntary embrace and had her back to me, but I had gripped her arms from behind and was holding them firmly. The trembling of her body gave me the impression that this was the result of the first real row she had had with Anthony and it was clear that the advent of Gloria, and not the absence of Aunt Eglantine, was the root cause of her agitation. 'And what do *you* want?' Anthony said to me.

'Only to receive your permission to go into the town and detach

Miss Brockworth from any elephants and steam-rollers she may have acquired in the supermarket,' I said, releasing Celia, who immediately flung herself out of the room. 'What the hell has got into the two of you?' I added seriously, as the door closed with a bang. 'What's happened to the turtle-dovery?'

He took me by the sleeve and walked me over to the window. The effects of the storm were apparent. Leaves and branches strewed the lawn; there were great pools of water and one or two roof-tiles lay on the broad path.

'It's that bitch,' he said. 'There's always trouble when she shows up anywhere. I nearly killed my closest friend once because of her. If you're really going into the town, you had better go at once. I'll give Celia a bit of time to cool off, and then I'll go and make my peace with her. It was rotten of me to joke about Aunt Eglantine. I'm very fond of the old nuisance-value, as a matter of fact.'

'It's a pity she's got this thing about witchcraft, isn't it? Makes her seem – well – ' I said delicately.

'Yes. She was telling me that Gloria is a black witch and Dame Beatrice a white one. She is convinced that Gloria conjured up last night's storm and got Roland and Kay bogged down because they laughed when Aunt Eglantine lobbed the lump of dough into Gloria's soup. She's sure that, if she attends the clinic, Dame Beatrice will preserve her from Gloria's vengeance. Personally, if I had been Gloria I would have poured what remained of the soup all over the old pest's topknot.'

'Better not say so in public. Oh, well, I'll be off, then.'

But I was not to go quite so soon as I expected. In fact, that morning I was not to go into the town at all. Coberley, who, with the lovely Marigold, was still at the school, rang up to say that he and his wife would not be coming over for lunch, as Marigold had slipped on the front steps of the school house (which meant the headmaster's private domicile) and had hit her head. He had sent for the doctor, as he thought she had slight concussion and had badly bruised the side of her face.

This news would not have kept me from going to look for Aunt

Eglantine and, in any case, I did not receive it until after my return to the house. I went to get my car, but as I walked past the old house I heard cries for help. The front door was closed, but I knew of the broken window at the back, so I shouted, 'I'm coming,' and went round there. The whole sash-window pane was out, so I climbed in and went along the passage.

Aunt Eglantine was lying amid the débris of the staircase. It was obvious what had happened. The old fathead, who must have weighed every bit of fourteen stone, had attempted to climb the stairs which Coberley had told me were totally unsafe. They had collapsed when she was halfway up and she had come down with a bang and had broken her left leg.

'Don't move,' I said. 'I'll get an ambulance.'

'Good Lord, whatever next!' shouted Anthony, when I had blurted out the news. The ambulance removed Aunt Eglantine to hospital and then I heard about Marigold's accident. Celia had been over to see her after she had returned from accompanying her aunt to the hospital.

'Marigold does have slight concussion,' she said, 'and is to be kept quiet.'

'Is her face much damaged?' I asked. It was monstrous that such beauty should be flawed, even temporarily.

'Well, it does look a bit of a mess,' Celia admitted. 'She seems to have scraped it on some rough stonework. It looks to me like a case for plastic surgery. Cranford Coberley is nearly out of his mind. He has threatened to flog every boy in the school if the culprit doesn't own up.'

'Own up to what?' I asked. 'Surely no boy is suspected of having pushed Mrs Coberley down the front steps? I expect they were simply slippery after all that rain.'

'It wasn't that. There's a covered way up to the front door. Somebody had spread butter on the top two steps, that's what.'

'But it's not all that easy for a boy to get hold of enough butter to spread it over two steps,' I pointed out.

'They are allowed to go into the town on Saturday mornings after early prep, and all the little devils have pocket money, I suppose,' said

Anthony. 'I'm surprised, though, that any of them should have played such a stupid and dangerous trick on the Coberleys. I don't know what the boys think of *him*, but I've always had the impression that Marigold was very popular with them.'

'You had better go over there and try to make him see reason. He can't flog the whole school,' said Celia. 'It's the height of barbarism to flog anybody, in my opinion, and certainly the innocent should not be punished.'

'How did you leave Aunt Eglantine?' asked Anthony.

'As comfortable as can be expected. I'm sorry for the nurses, that's all.'

'Did you travel with her in the ambulance?'

'No, I followed it in my mini. By the way, be sure to keep the garage locked up. I saw two police cars turning into the road which leads to the old convent, so on my way back I drove up there to find out what was happening. A policeman stopped me and said the way was blocked by a burnt-out car.

' "Nobody hurt, and no number plates," he told me. They think it was a stolen car which the thieves had abandoned. I suppose they had removed the number plates to baffle the police.'

'It would hardly do that. Somebody is sure to report a stolen car, but why burn it?' I said.

'Just bloody-mindedness,' said Anthony.

6
Arson

The first upshot of the butter affair was bizarre if not instructive. To pacify Celia and help him to get himself reinstated in her good graces, Anthony went over to the school to reason with Coberley, only to find that his arguments had been used already by Marigold herself. He came back with the story.

'Marigold wouldn't have it that any boy was guilty,' he said. 'She had a curious story to tell. She had been standing at the sitting-room window when she heard a voice call out, "Oh, Mrs Coberley, a goat is eating your kitchen garden!" '

The school, it appeared, had a number of pet animals looked after by the boys, so Marigold ran out and immediately took her nasty toss down the steps. Coberley's inquisition of his pupils had not produced a culprit and he had issued his threat in the heat of the moment.

When Anthony met him he was already beginning to simmer down. He said that he had instituted enquiries among his staff and it appeared that no boy had been missing from lessons or from games at any time, and the headmaster's house was strictly out of bounds. He was telling Anthony this when there was a knock on the door of his sanctum and a small, pale boy wearing spectacles came in. The dialogue had run as follows:

'Well, Duckett?'

'Please, sir, I've come to confess, sir.'

'Who sent you?'

'Please, sir, Robson and the other prefects, sir.'

'To confess to what, Duckett?'

'Please, sir, that I buttered the steps.'

'*You?*'

'Yes, sir, please, sir.'

'I find this incredible. *Did* you butter the steps?'

'Please, sir, no, sir, but Robson said it was right that one man should die for the people.'

'Did he, indeed?' Upon this (Anthony said), Coberley rang the bell and sent a servant to find Robson – 'he should be with Mr Stace in B room' – and bring him to the headmaster. Soon a handsome child of about thirteen appeared.

'You sent for me, sir?'

'Yes, Robson. Duckett, you may go. Now, Robson, what is all this I hear? (Robson, Mr Wotton, is my head boy.)'

'How do you do, sir.' He and Anthony shook hands.

'Now, Robson, explain yourself. I know you too well to believe that you would wantonly offer me a lamb such as Duckett for the slaughter. You must have had a good reason.'

'Oh, sir, yes, sir. We knew you would not beat a little boy like Duckett, sir, so we thought he was the best one to send, being delicate and wearing glasses.'

'Duckett did not butter the steps, then?'

'No, sir, of course not, sir. Nobody did.'

'Then how came the steps to be buttered?'

'I don't know, sir. We're sure none of our men did it. That's what I meant, sir. I mean, sir, we wouldn't, would we?'

'How can I be sure of that?' It was clear, said Anthony, that the head boy was a privileged person, 'as it is right and proper that a head boy should be,' he added.

'Well, nobody would want to hurt Mrs Coberley, would they, sir? Besides, if chaps have got money, they wouldn't spend it on butter; they would spend it on things like doughnuts, wouldn't they, sir?'

'Very well. I shall suspend judgment *sine die*. Do you know what that means?'

'Oh, yes, sir. My father is a QC.'

'You might do worse than follow in his footsteps.'

'I am going to be a psychologist, sir.'

'That might suit your undoubted gifts equally well. All right. Be off with you.'

'They size you up, don't they?' said Anthony, when the lad had gone. 'He needn't worry about "going to be a psychologist". He is one already.'

'They all are,' said Coberley.

'It wasn't a boy's voice which Marigold heard,' said Celia, when Anthony reported the visit.

'So she appears to have told Coberley. Anyway, he is taking no action for the present. He is beginning to think it might have been the work of town hooligans. He caught two of them a few months ago trying to steal the couple of geese the boys keep as pets.'

The affair might have remained at that, but for a report from Aunt Eglantine. Celia visited her in hospital and came back with the story. The elderly lady had had no intention of going into the town on the morning of her accident. She had popped downstairs to pick up the tray of coffee and toast and at about ten o'clock she had gone to the old house 'to look at the picture you said was a Rubens,' she told Celia. She had tried the front door, discovered, of course, that she could not get in, so had gone round to the back and found the broken window. She demolished the rest of it so that the aperture was wide enough to accept her bulk, 'and then that creature came along and helped me in. She is stronger than she looks,' she said.

'Did you expect to see her?' Celia asked.

'Yes and no.'

'What does that mean?'

'That silly couple who bogged their car down said she was there in the old house, but I thought she might have gone.'

'She must have slept there. I wonder what she did for food and bedding?' Celia had said. 'There was nobody in the house when Anthony went over yesterday, though.'

'I suppose she didn't want anybody to know she was there. She asked me why I had come. I told her I wanted to see a picture,' Aunt Eglantine had continued. 'She said that she had taken it upstairs, as people could get into the house and she did not want it stolen. I did not

48

believe her when she declared it was her property, and I looked in all the downstairs rooms to find it, but it wasn't there. She said that if I wanted to see it I would have to mount the stairs.'

Apparently Aunt Eglantine had decided, very rashly, to do this, but rickety stairs which might have sustained Gloria's meagre frame proved unequal to the old lady's much greater weight and she had come crashing down.

'And Gloria left her lying there,' said Celia, telling us the story in a voice that trembled. 'Left her lying there in the hall with a broken leg, and slammed the front door after herself with poor Aunt unable to get any help until Corin found her. I never heard of anything more callous.'

After I had found Aunt Eglantine lying amid the ruins of the staircase and had run back to the house, I had left the front door on the catch so that the ambulance men could get in. After they had removed the old lady to hospital I had gone back to have a look round. The nail on which the picture had hung was still there, and so was the patch on the wall where the picture had shielded the wallpaper from the sun, but the picture itself had disappeared. Whether Gloria really had braved the dangerous staircase and taken the picture upstairs, or whether she had made off with it, there was no way of telling at that juncture.

Anthony sent in his gardener to clear up the mess. 'Make sure you leave room to get the front door open again,' he said to the man. 'Tomorrow I'll have to hire a truck and get all the muck taken down to the council dump. We can't deal with it here.'

'Make a nice bonfire and help me burn a lot of garden rubbish which I got piling up, Mr Wotton, eh, sir?'

'Oh, all right, then. Leave it until tomorrow and I'll come and give you a hand.'

'If I split up the big pieces of wood, sir, I reckon a couple of wheelbarrows would shift it.'

'Means several journeys. Make it three wheelbarrows,' I said, 'if you know where to borrow an extra one.'

'Thanks, Corin,' said Anthony. 'We've got two and Coberley will lend me another.'

However, it rained all the next day, so the heap of wood remained *in situ*, except that the gardener and his son, a lad of about fourteen who, I'm pretty sure, ought to have been in school, split up the woodwork of the staircase into manageable lengths and piled it up in the hall. When Anthony and I went over there in waterproofs and tweed hats, the result looked like an unlighted funeral pyre.

Now that Aunt Eglantine was in hospital, I was the only guest left in the house, so I suggested that it was about time I went, too. Anthony, echoed by Celia, vetoed this.

'Nonsense,' he said. 'I know you were only invited to stay for a week, but we need you here. Are you tired of our company already?'

'No, of course not,' I said, 'but with all the upsets – well, *you* know.'

'What upsets?' he said. 'Some ill-natured lout smears grease on stone steps and an unsuspecting woman comes a cropper, but it didn't happen here and is no business of ours. A silly old lady who ought to have had more sense elects to climb an obviously unsafe staircase and breaks a limb. That didn't happen here, either. Two young idiots choose an impassable lane in torrential rain, get bogged down, and one of them catches a nasty cold. *That* didn't happen here. The one incident which *did* happen here – deplorable though it was from some aspects – turned out well. It rid us of Gloria Mundy.'

He spoke too soon. We were not rid of Gloria Mundy, not by a long chalk. I found afterwards that I remembered the evening well. The rain had eased off again at Thursday lunchtime, so I had spent the afternoon cruising around in my car. It was pleasant to get out into the countryside after having been confined to the house because of the return of the wet weather. I took the long hill up to Rodborough and then drove across the high, flat, seemingly boundless expanse of the common, had a look at the Long Stone and so on to Minchinhampton, with its seventeenth-century pillared market hall.

From here I went on to Nailsworth, crossed westwards over a pre-historic landscape with a tumulus and a long barrow on it and then swung north to Nympsfield. I had plenty of time in hand, so, instead of going straight back to Beeches Lawn, I turned south again to get a glimpse of Owlpen manor house and then went on to Uley.

I left the car at the roadside, called at a cottage for the key and the candle which were kept there – nobody was in, but the key, the candle and a box of matches were there for the borrowing – then I made my way on foot to the long barrow known locally as Hetty Pegler's Tump.

This involved a walk on a rough but well-trodden path alongside a big field. The path was bordered by bushes on the right-hand side, but my objective was straight ahead of me and could not be missed. I went up to it, carrying my candle, matches and the key, and looked doubt-fully at the very low wooden doorway with which the Ministry of Works had replaced the original neolithic stone portal, and decided not to make use of the key after all.

My shoes were already muddy and almost soaked through, and I could see no way of insinuating myself into the tomb without getting my clothes covered in mud, for to get inside the long barrow involved, so far as I could determine, crawling in on hands and knees.

However, the view from Hetty Pegler was well worth the visit. Like other long barrows – I am thinking particularly of Belas Knap on Cleeve Cloud – Hetty Pegler's Tump was high up and furnished the widest possible views except those gained from an aeroplane. Particularly there was the gleam of silver which I knew was the Severn and I could even make out the Welsh mountains on the other side of it, and, nearer at hand, the dips and slopes and autumn colouring of the wolds.

I returned the key, candle and matches and drove back to Beeches Lawn by a hilly, wooded road which writhed about, but took me to the railway station and so home. We dined earlier than usual that evening. I was missing the other guests, but it was what people call 'a good miss'. I am not a very sociable man, preferring, as I do, my own com-pany to that of others. In this case, moreover, none of the house-party, with the exception of Dame Beatrice, had appealed to me much, although I would have made an exception in favour of Marigold Coberley. However, her husband had guarded her with such a jealous eye that it was difficult even to get speech with her, let alone the tête-à-tête I would have liked.

After dinner Anthony said he had a vestry meeting and left us. Celia refused to have the drawing-room curtains drawn, although those in the dining-room had been closed. She said there would be what she called 'a stormy sunset' and she wanted to enjoy it. The drawing-room was exceptionally large. It had a huge bay window with china cabinets built in on either side and in the same wall there was a glass-topped door which opened on to the path round the lawn. On one side of the fireplace there were shelves for bric-à-brac and on the other side there was another window from which the copper beech tree dominated the outlook. I stood at this window and thought how pleasant domesticity could be.

There was a long ridge of low-lying cloud behind the hills and the evening light which came in through the big bay window to my right threw lurid colour from the setting sun on to the further wall. Celia wanted to go up on to the roof to get a fuller view of the sunset, but I demurred at first. It would be chilly up there, I said, and, after the rain, the leads would be slippery and could be dangerous. I reminded her of Marigold's accident.

However, she insisted, so we put on wraps, climbed the stairs and went along a passage to where a trap-door and a loft ladder could take us on to the flat part of the roof.

'Hullo,' said Celia, when we had emerged. 'Where's all that smoke coming from? Something must be on fire.'

'Perhaps your gardener is having his bonfire without waiting for our help,' I said.

'Nonsense, Corin! It's the old house!'

It was fortunate that the town was so near. The fire brigade reached us in a matter of minutes. I left Celia in the house and went along to see the conflagration. The old house was a mass of flames. There was billowing smoke and crackling wood and, although the fire brigade soon had the situation under control, the damage was done and where the old house had stood there soon remained nothing but a charred mess of burnt wood deluged with water and the grim skeleton of blackened walls.

'So much for that,' said Celia, when I told her, but there was more, far more, to come.

'Was the property insured?' I asked Anthony when he returned to the house. He said that it was, but only the fabric itself, as any furniture had been moved out long ago.

'What I can't make out,' he went on, 'is how the fire started, especially after all the rain we've had.'

'Hooligans. Probably the same gang as were responsible for Mrs Coberley's accident, don't you think?'

'If so, it's a police matter. I shall see to it that every enquiry is made. An empty house does not go up in flames because of internal combustion.'

'I suppose – I mean, Miss Brockworth did tell us that she had met Miss Mundy in there,' I said tentatively.

'Oh, Aunt Eglantine will say anything which comes into her head. She is not to be relied on. I'm sure Gloria was far enough away before Aunt climbed into the house and had her accident when the staircase collapsed. The old nuisance has a bee in her bonnet. She didn't meet the girl there. All the same, the house must have been set on fire deliberately and I'm going to find out who did it. It was just a piece of wanton destruction on a par with all the other lawless, senseless behaviour which goes on nowadays, and somehow it's got to be stopped.'

'Easier said than done,' I remarked. 'In these cases of wilful damage by louts the police seem to be helpless.'

However, they were not so helpless as to ignore a most grievous occurrence which was the aftermath of the fire. What hit us next day was the appalling news that a body had been found among the charred embers of the old house.

The news was brought by the gardener. He came up to the house early next morning and asked to see Anthony. Anthony was busy. He was one of the churchwardens of a church in the town and he and his companion-in-office had planned to go over the church accounts before they submitted them to the usual auditors, so he told the maid who came with the message to refer the gardener to Celia.

I knew about this because I was with Celia at the time. We were in the little garden room to which he already had brought some fine hot-house chrysanthemums for the vases. I was stripping the lower leaves from the tall, woody stems and getting in some gentle tapping on them with a light hammer, and she was doing the flower arrangements. The gardener, who had been kept at the back door while the maid apprised Anthony of his arrival, was shown into the garden room on Anthony's orders.

'I'm sorry, mum,' he said, twisting his tweed hat in his enormous hands, 'but I aimed to have spoke to the master.'

'He is too busy to see you, Platt. What do you want?'

'He didn't ought to be too busy to see me if he knowed what I come about.'

'Well, you can tell me what you have come about and I will let him know what it is as soon as he is free.'

'It's about the old house, mum. Something us found there, me and the lad.'

'Well, what was it?'

'Beg pardon, mum, but it's for the master, not you, if you'll excuse me. There's something as the fire chief and me think as he ought to see.'

'Oh, get on with it, Platt! What is it?'

Even then it did not occur to me, nor, I am sure, to Celia, that he was talking about a burnt and blackened corpse which he had found among the ashes.

7
Ichabod

This shocking news brought along the police, of course. Anthony's complaint about destructive hooligans went by the board in the face of this far more serious issue. According to the firemen, petrol or paraffin must have been poured over the heap of chopped-up timber in the hall for the house to have burnt so fiercely.

'If only we'd moved the stuff out instead of my taking time off to go out in my car to visit Hetty Pegler's Tump!' I said remorsefully.

'Nonsense, my dear chap. I put the job off myself because I wanted the fallen leaves swept off the lawn. But this business is the very devil. One of the wretched gang of youths who thought they would amuse themselves by setting fire to the place must have been trapped by the flames or overcome by the smoke, and his mates ran off and left him to it.'

It turned out to be even worse than that. The fire must have been started with the deliberate intention of covering up a murder, and the corpse was not that of a boy, but of a woman.

We did not know this at first. At the preliminary interview which Anthony had, the uniformed inspector who called took a most unexpected line. I was not present, of course, but got a full account later. The inspector asked whether Anthony had ever suspected that the old house had been taken over by squatters.

'Most certainly not,' my friend replied. 'The house was quite unfit for human habitation. Besides, I have had an offer for it from somebody who was prepared to do it up – the headmaster of the preparatory school next door. He has been inside it more than half a dozen times during the past month or so and would have informed me at once of any tenants. Apart from that, my gardener would have known if anybody had been living there. Besides, I myself passed the house every time I went to the garage for my car. What makes you ask about squatters?'

'In a corner of the cellar which the fire had hardly reached we found empty tins which had contained food and beer, sir.'

'Sounds more like a passing tramp. Anyway, I'm certain the house had not been taken over by squatters.'

'Have you missed any food lately?'

'You had better ask my cook. She has made no mention of anything missing from her stores.'

'Oh, well, that can wait, sir. I mentioned we have evidence that the house was occupied. I take it you have heard of the body discovered among the débris?'

'My wife would hardly have telephoned you if we had not. The body must be that of some unfortunate tramp, or one of the fire-raisers who didn't get away in time. A truly dreadful business, Inspector, and I'm glad the body was removed before I saw it.'

'I'm afraid I shall have to ask you to take a look at it, sir. The fire was not the cause of death. We are investigating a case of wilful murder. There will be a pathologist's report, but our own police surgeon says that accident or suicide can be ruled out. Our immediate aim is to get the dead person identified. That is partly why I asked whether you had been aware that you had squatters on your premises. Now, in the face of your denials, it's a long shot, I know, but I would like you to accompany me to the mortuary to see whether you can identify the corpse, as your gardener informs me you had people staying here.'

'But my denials are absolute. I can't possibly help you. I assure you that I have never known that anybody was occupying the old place, let alone ever having seen anybody there. As for my guests, they all left safely and can be accounted for. The only one who is still here is Mr Stratford and he is hale and hearty enough.'

'And you are sure there were no squatters?'

'Only a few days ago some friends of mine went in to look at a portrait which had hung in one of the downstairs rooms for years. They would most certainly have told me if they had suspected that the house was occupied. The headmaster who has an option to purchase was one of them – he has a key. As I told you, I'm sure he would have known if squatters had taken over the building. No, no, a gang of young hooligans is far more likely and I should not be able to recognise any of them.'

'Just so, sir. All the same, I would like you to take a look at the body that was found. We need to get it identified.'

'But how the hell can I identify a person who was entirely unknown to me?'

'The body was found on your premises, sir. This is more like an elimination than an identification.'

'Elimination? Oh, but, dammit, look here – !'

'I'm afraid I must insist, sir.'

'Is the body – well, is it, as it were, very badly – er – ?'

'You need take only a quick look, sir. There is one special feature which may help with identification. It should be sufficient for our purpose.'

'May Mr Stratford come with me? He has been staying in the house, as I told you, and is still here.'

'We may be glad of him for confirmation, sir. Are there no other persons in the house?'

'Two women servants and my wife, but I'm not going to have them look at any dead bodies.'

'We would be loth to submit females to such an ordeal, sir.'

'If you think this person was a squatter and as I have assured you, I know nothing of any such, what is the point of taking me along to look at this body of yours? I repeat that I cannot help you.'

'A matter of routine, sir, as the corpse was found under very suspicious circumstances on premises belonging to you, as I have explained. The singular feature to which I alluded should settle the matter of identification if the person should turn out to be somebody you know.'

I had been uneasy in my mind ever since the inspector's arrival and when Anthony told me of this reference (the second one) to what the police seemed to think was an unmistakeable feature, my thoughts went to the red and black hair of Gloria Mundy, that uninvited and unwelcome interloper. The same idea presented itself to Anthony, I think, for he said in an aside to me after I had been sent for, '*Je pense que les gendarmes ont quelque chose debout leur manche.*'

I nodded. The inspector smiled and said, 'I ought to tell you that I understand French, sir. Even yours,' he added unkindly, 'and I assure you that we have nothing up our sleeve. Shall we go, sir? You and Mr Stratford will be shown the body separately, of course.'

'I must let my wife know where I am going.'

'Of course, sir.'

We went in a police car. Nothing was said on the journey. What Anthony's thoughts were I do not know. Personally I was nerving myself for what I knew would be the most unpleasant experience of my life. At the same time I was aware of a sick sort of curiosity of which I was ashamed but could not dismiss.

Anthony was first and they let him out by another door, for I saw nothing of him before it was my turn. The mortuary smelt heavily of disinfectant, an odour I detest, and it did not help my already queasy stomach.

'Just a glance, sir,' said the inspector encouragingly. 'Nothing to worry about.'

Sez you! I thought grimly, swallowing in order to rid myself of my horrid feeling of nausea. The attendant drew back the sheet from the face, or what had been the face. It was blackened and quite unrecognisable. The feature referred to twice by the inspector was only too plain to see, however. On the otherwise unidentifiable head of the corpse was the slightly scorched red and black hair which was what I thought of as the trademark of Gloria Mundy. The inspector covered up the horror which lay on the mortuary slab and led me away from it.

'Well, sir?' he said, with a briskness which I suppose was an indication that I must pull myself together.

'Well,' I said, 'I don't know, I'm sure. It's – there's nothing to go on but the hair, and that doesn't make sense, does it?'

'No, sir?'

'I mean, if the head is – is like that, the hair ought to be shrivelled right up and you wouldn't see the two colours and all that, would you?'

'Your guess is as good as mine, sir, so if I may know what your verdict is?'

'Oh, the identification. I suppose the body is that of Gloria Mundy, but –'

'You need go no further, sir. Thank you for your help.'

All was not yet over. We were taken to the police station, where Anthony was escorted to the interview room and I was given a seat opposite the desk sergeant's counter. He asked me whether I would like a cup of tea. I thought this apparently kind suggestion was an indication that I might need to be fortified against my next ordeal.

I refused the tea and asked whether I had long to wait. He answered, in the elliptical manner of which the police are pastmasters, that these things took a little time. He offered me a newspaper to read.

I took it and thanked him, but it is hardly necessary to say that, although I looked at it for courtesy's sake, I did not read a single word. I was still wondering what Anthony had thought when he was shown Gloria's hair and her ravaged face, and what he was saying at that moment in the interview room.

At last it was my turn. They led Anthony past me and saw him out and then a constable touched me on the arm and said, 'This way, sir.' In the interview room he positioned himself against the door. The inspector was not there. A mild-looking man in plain clothes gave me a seat opposite him at a table, drew a writing-pad towards himself, took up a ballpoint and said, with what I thought (with even worse misgivings than before) was a kind of gruesome cheerfulness, 'Well, now, sir, let's get down to the nitty-gritty, shall we? Then we can both have our lunch.'

'I suppose it's no good to ask you what my friend has told you,' I said.

'The same as I hope you are going to tell me, sir. You say that you recognised the body as being that of a Miss Gloria Mundy. How well did you know her?'

'Only well enough to recognise her rather unusual two-coloured hair. She was my fellow guest at lunch a few days ago.'

'The lunch being where, sir?'

'At Mr Wotton's house. I had been invited to pay him a visit and Miss Mundy turned up unexpectedly and was offered lunch. She took umbrage at the table manners of another guest and left before the end of the meal. I never saw her alive again, and I had never met her before that day.'

He pushed a writing-pad towards me. Another plain-clothes man had been making notes at a small table in a corner of the room.

'Would you read what the detective-sergeant has written down, sir, and sign it as a true report of what you have told me?'

That was all. I was thanked – the deadly courtesy of the English police is far more terrifying than the bullying methods adopted by some other Forces – and Anthony and I were driven back to Beeches Lawn. Celia was anxious to know what had happened.

'I don't like it,' she said, when she heard what Anthony had to say. 'As for that awful Gloria, if she had been camping out there, some-body would have seen her and told us. What about Platt and the boy who helps him in the garden?'

'They can't have seen anybody, or they would have mentioned it. All the same, the police found empty tins in the cellar to back up their story about squatters. Now we know it was Gloria, she *must* have been living there.'

'Those things could have been down there for years. There's no water or lighting or sanitation in the old house. People couldn't live there. The dreadful thing is that, if there were no squatters, somebody else killed Gloria. You and Corin had to say you knew her. They'll probe – the police, I mean – and goodness knows what they'll come up with. How well *did* you know her?'

'I told you ages ago. I had a lighthearted flirtation with her. It was nothing more. I met her on a Mediterranean cruise. She only wanted to get free drinks on board and her shore outings paid for. I was the unattached member of my party, so I went along with her.'

'Old Hara-kiri seems to have had the same sort of experience,' I said,

60

backing him up. 'Gloria seems to have been adept at picking out the suckers,' I added, less graciously.

'And what about you?' asked Celia, resenting, as I had guessed she would, my slighting reference to her husband.

'Me?' I said. 'I don't like skinny wenches. When I take a girl I want an armful. To get back to the point at issue, what happens next? If squatters are out of it, perhaps Anthony was unwise to stick to the story that there was nobody camping out in the old house.'

'Oh, they'll question the gardeners and the tradesmen, I suppose,' said Celia. 'I hope they won't bother poor old Aunt Eglantine while she's in hospital.'

'If she had been minding her own business instead of breaking into empty houses and climbing rickety staircases, the meddling old so-and-so wouldn't *be* in hospital. And of course they'll question her,' said Anthony. 'What's more, they'll round up everybody else who has been staying in the house and was here when Gloria turned up to lunch. Our name will be a hissing and a by-word among our friends. "Don't, whatever you do, go and stay with the Wottons unless you want to be had up for murder". That's what will go around.'

'Don't be silly,' said Celia. 'This business is bad enough without your getting hysterical over it. Why on earth, when Gloria knew the place was on fire, didn't she run off? Could she have been drunk or drugged?'

'She had been stabbed. That much the police did let us know. She was dead, they think, before the fire started.'

'Then it was started to try to cover up the murder – or could it have been suicide?'

'According to what the chap told me in the interview room, the doctor thinks she was stabbed in the back.'

'That being so,' I said, 'a thought occurs to me. Most probably she wasn't killed in the old house at all. She could have been murdered elsewhere, the body brought to the old house and the fire started to cover up the crime, as Celia says.'

'But who would have known that the old house was available and that there was a pile of chopped wood waiting to be made into a bonfire?' Anthony demanded. 'If you ask me, I'm in the devil of a spot. I gave the order for the wood of the staircase to be chopped up; it was my house, and I knew Gloria from the old days and had ditched her and, like the bad penny she was, she bobbed up again. I might have had a very good reason to get rid of her – or so the police will think.'

'She was in your house for less than a couple of hours,' I said. 'I saw her arrive, you know.'

'And how long is it going to take the police to find out that she was the cause of a first-class row between Celia and me?'

'How *can* they find out? Neither of you will tell them, and I certainly shan't,' I said. 'Besides, it wasn't a first-class row; just a border skirmish such as all married couples indulge in from time to time. You're fretting unnecessarily, old man.'

'One never knows what the servants may have overheard,' said Celia, 'and we did go it rather hammer and tongs after you had left the room, Corin, and again in bed. They say the walls have ears, so I think there is some cause for worry, although not as much as Anthony believes.'

'The detective-superintendent at the police station asked me for the names of everybody who had been staying in the house during the past week,' said Anthony. 'That's why I said they are certain to question Aunt Eglantine. She claims to have seen Gloria in the old house and so do those two youngsters. McMaster saw her in the grounds, too, so we know she couldn't have left when we thought she did.'

'Proves that Gloria was alive at those times,' I said.

'A fat lot of use *that's* going to be,' Anthony retorted. 'Oh, well, nothing for us to do but wait for the inquest, I suppose. You'll have to stay on for a bit longer, Corin, as the police seem to have involved you in the beastly business.'

'We shall be thankful to have you,' said Celia.

'But I've got a job to finish for old Hara-kiri,' I protested. 'I *can't* stay here much longer.'

'You may have no option, old man, until this business is cleared up,' said Anthony.

'You wouldn't desert us at a time like this, would you?' said Celia. Anthony kicked the leg of a chair.

'What a hell of a nuisance that girl is!' he said. 'She was a hell of a nuisance when she was alive and she's the hell of a nuisance now she's dead. I don't like that inspector's manner and I didn't like that chap who interviewed me at the police station. They'll ferret around and uncover things.'

'Such as your little, short-lived affair with Gloria?' I said. 'Don't be an ass, man! You weren't the only one. What about Hara-kiri? And, from what I gather, there could have been a dozen men that she'd had on the hook at some time or other.'

'She wasn't killed on their premises, though. That's the rub. She turned up here, left in a huff because of Aunt Eg's inexcusable behaviour and then somebody killed her.'

'Well, nobody killed her without a motive.'

'But I *had* a motive, Corin. She came here with the intention of blackmailing me. She wanted to give up her job and go abroad. She told me so almost as soon as she arrived. That's why she came for money.'

'Did she threaten you? And did anybody overhear the conversation?'

'She made her intention quite plain. The interview was only between the two of us, but I don't suppose I moderated my voice. I don't when I lose my temper, and lose my temper I did.'

'What sort of job did she do?'

'She was a sales assistant at that fashion shop called Trends.'

'How could she afford a cruise that other time?'

'It was a one-class boat and she had a cabin right down in the depths. That's why I let her share mine, on the strict QT.'

'Why didn't you kick her out of the house straight away that day? Why ask her to stay to lunch?'

'I did that,' said Celia. 'I was curious about her. I wanted to find out what Anthony had ever seen in her.'

'Nothing, of course,' said Anthony morosely. 'I never saw anything in her. She just happened, like any other disaster.'

'But she couldn't have blackmailed you merely on the strength of a ship-board flirtation. What else have you got on your conscience?' asked Celia.

'Nothing, of course.' But to me his denial did not ring true and I was worried. I tried another tack – or, rather, I returned to one we had tried earlier.

'Look, ' I said, 'there's nothing to show that she was killed in the old house. Let's sort this out a bit. At least two days elapsed between the time Aunt Eglantine saw her and the time the body was found after the fire. She couldn't have been living in the old house without somebody knowing she was still there. She could have been killed – mugged, as likely as not — anywhere in the neighbourhood and the body brought back here and the fire started to cover up the murder. What's wrong with that theory? It seems utterly likely to me.'

'Why should they bring her back here?'

'Oh, for goodness' sake, man!' I said desperately. 'They knew the old house, of course. Plenty of people would know of it.' But he would look on nothing but the black side and I went to bed a very depressed man. There must be something which he had not told me. I racked my brains, but could not imagine what it was.

8
Hounds in Cry

I think all three of us dreaded Anthony's appearance in the coroner's court. He and the medical witnesses were called and then the police put up two other people, one of whom I had more or less expected, the other somewhat of a surprise. The chief fireman was the first of them to take the stand. He described the fire, referred to Celia's telephone call to the fire brigade and, in answer to questions he stated that, to the best of his knowledge, there had been no body among the ashes and nobody had been trapped in the house.

'She would have run out screaming if she had been in there when the fire started,' he said, 'if she had been alive, that is, which we're told she wasn't, but we would have seen her body. Wood burns out to fine ash, as everybody knows, and wood – plenty of it, of course, but that makes no difference – was all that got burnt up, the walls being good Cotswold stone and still standing.'

'What about the roof? That wasn't made of wood,' said the coroner.

'Oh, well, yes, a lot of slates did come down, but if there had been a body I still reckon me or some of my lads would have seen it.' (This point was emphasised by the police surgeon, who asserted that the body showed no sign of having been struck by falling roof-tiles.)

The surprise witness, so far as I was concerned, was Anthony's gardener, who had reported the finding of the body. I suppose my surprise was irrational.

'You are William George Platt?'

'That's me.'

'You live at Begonia Cottage, Hilcombury?'

'That's right, there being no gardener's cottage on the estate, so I go to Beeches Lawn daily.'

'So you were not at Beeches Lawn when the fire broke out in what is known as the old house?'

'A man can't be expected to do no gardening after dark.'

'Where were you?'

'At the Weaver and Loom. Plenty there to say so.'

'When did you know about the fire?'

'Next morning, when I went to put in my day.'

'Did nobody mention the fire to you before that?'

'Ah, come to think of it, they did, well, sort of. When I got home from the pub my missus said as she had heard the fire-engines go past our cottage, so she wondered where the fire was, or whether it was only an exercise, but it was no business of ourn, we didn't think, so we went to bed and then next morning I found that poor soul when I see what had happened to the old house. I started to do a bit of clearing up and then I seen her and went to get my orders from Mr Wotton who I guessed would be having his breakfast.'

'And when you had reported to Mr Wotton?'

'I never. He was busy, so I reported to Mrs Wotton and I reckon she phoned the police.'

'Did you, in your capacity as gardener, ever store any inflammable material in the old house?'

' 'Course not. I've got my shed and anyway the old house was kept locked. I only got in to see the body because the front door, being wood, was burnt down.'

'And you had no idea that anybody was living in the old house?'

'I'd soon have had 'em out of it. If anybody lived there, they only lived there of a night.'

The inquest had to be adjourned so that the police could continue with their enquiries, but everybody, ourselves included, had expected this. Poor old Anthony had had to say that he had identified the body as being that of Gloria Mundy, for no relatives had come forward, neither had the police been able to find any, for any personal documents which might have been helpful and which might have been in

Gloria's handbag or suitcase had been consumed in the fire.

The medical evidence did not help the police very much, either. The report was that it was impossible to state the time when the murder had been committed, for all the usual indications – staining and discoloration spreading into the face and neck, marbling of the veins and so forth, had been eliminated by the scorching that the body, and particularly the face, had received in the fire.

One thing was certain. The fire itself was not the cause of death. There was clear evidence of a deep stab wound, inflicted in the back, which must have killed the girl. The fire had undoubtedly been an attempt to cover up this more serious crime. What seemed to me to be the most extraordinary feature of the case – the fact that, although the face was unrecognisible, the hair had been no more than scorched – was not mentioned, so I suspected that the police were keeping very quiet about this possibly significant circumstance.

The inquest had opened at ten in the morning. Celia had not attended it, but, apart from Anthony and myself, William Underedge had turned up, although he slipped away so quickly at the end that we did not get a chance to speak to him. I wondered how he had found out the date and time of the inquest, but I supposed Celia had written to Karen and the news had been passed on.

We had scarcely finished lunch that day when Detective-Inspector Rouse and Detective-Sergeant Skinner were announced. Their purpose, it seemed, was to confirm who had been staying in the house when Gloria first turned up.

'You see, sir,' said Rouse, 'the medical evidence, as it stands, is of very little use to us for the time being. As I read the pathologist's report, the deceased could have been killed almost as soon as she arrived here.

'We know, from your own admission, when that was, and the head-master of the school, Mr Coberley, and also his wife, whom I interviewed separately – her in the nursing home – before I came here, both confirm it, but I need witnesses who can tell me of subsequent events. As I see it, the deceased could have met her death at any time from that day almost up to the time when the body was actually put into the house and the bonfire started.'

Anthony confirmed the list of names and addresses he had given before, then he and Celia were politely but very definitely dismissed and Rouse turned his attention to me.

'Now, sir, obviously Miss Mundy was acquainted with Mr and Mrs Wotton, or she would hardly have turned up at this house and been invited to stay for lunch.'

'I don't think Mrs Wotton knew her,' I said, 'although it was she who issued the invitation. I believe Miss Mundy was acquainted with Anthony Wotton before his marriage, that's all.'

I wondered, even as I said this, whether I was not letting Anthony down, but I did not see why Celia should be mixed up in this beastly affair more than could be helped. After all, I had had my arms round her, however involuntary the embrace had been on both sides, and the warmth of that sporadic encounter, together with her warm greeting upon my arrival at Beeches Lawn, remained with me. Besides, I thought of Imogen, whom I had allowed to slip out of my life.

Rouse pounced upon my words.

'So Mr Wotton was acquainted with the deceased, but Mrs Wotton was not,' he said. 'I see. May I ask whether you yourself were acquainted with the poor young woman?'

'No, I had never met her before she came here.'

'What about the other guests?'

I thought I saw a chance of doing a bit of cover-up for Anthony, whom I felt I might have landed in the cart.

'Well, there was another man who had known her some time back, I believe,' I said, 'but he wasn't actually present when she arrived and she had gone before he got here.' (I reserved the information that Hara-kiri had seen her in the grounds.)

'Who would that be, sir?'

A man named McMaster, H K McMaster. He and Wotton used to play in the first fifteen when we were at college together, so I suppose they knew the same people.' I thought rather well of myself for thinking that one up. He consulted Anthony's list.

'Mr McMaster, yes. Exactly when did he arrive and how long did he stay?'

'He came on the same day as Miss Mundy, but later. As a matter of fact, McMaster came to see *me*, to talk over some literary work I was doing for him. It was in preference to my going to see him at his home that the Wottons invited him to meet me here. Our talk was supposed to be completed that same afternoon, but the storm made all the roads pretty bad, so McMaster was asked to stay the night, and decided to do so.'

I hoped to goodness that he would not ask whether Hara-kiri had seen anything of Gloria in the grounds or elsewhere, and he did not. He merely asked whether any of the other guests had been acquainted with Gloria. Here, thinking that I could spread the load a little further, I said that I did not think any of the other guests had met her before, but then I added, 'But I believe one of the young couples, who had to come back because their car got bogged down when they were caught in the storm, thought they might have seen her. Of course they only got a fleeting glimpse of her in the rain and they didn't really know her.'

'Then why did they assume it was Miss Mundy?'

'That extraordinary hair by which Wotton and I identified the body.'

'Ah, yes, of course, sir. Where had they met her previously?'

'Only at Sunday lunch. By the way, is Dame Beatrice down on Wotton's list of guests? She was not at lunch but she had come to cast a professional eye over the dotty aunt, and she had gone before Gloria came. Had to attend a conference in Cheltenham, I think.'

'Dotty aunt?' said Rouse, and I could almost see him prick his ears. 'How dotty? Do you mean' – he looked at Anthony's list – 'Miss Brockworth?'

'Dotty enough to heave a chunk of bread into Miss Mundy's plate of soup and splash her up to the eyebrows, and dotty enough to attempt to climb an unsafe staircase and bring it down with her and break a leg,' I explained.

'That would be the staircase in the burnt-out house?'

'Yes. That's why there was all that wood to which somebody set fire.'

'Where is the lady now?'

'In hospital, of course.'

'And you think she is mentally unstable?'

'How else can you account for her actions?'

'I have her down on the list of guests with which Mr Wotton has furnished me. All the same, he did not mention the hospital or her accident. He merely gave me her home address.'

'I suppose that is what you asked for.'

'I don't approve of people who withhold information, sir. I shall have to see this old lady. If she went to the old house, she may have something to tell me.'

'Well, take care that you haven't got a plateful of soup in front of you. She's a dead shot at short range,' I said, with a flippancy which was not only out of place but, under the circumstances, unwise, for he said stiffly that he was obliged to me for the warning. I asked whether there was anything more I could do for him. He replied that he had no more questions for me 'at the moment'.

I did not care for the sound of this. It was clear that he had not finished with me. I pressed the point and asked whether I was free to return home.

'At least, not home,' I said. 'I want to carry out my commission for Mr McMaster and he has set a deadline.' I explained the nature of the job I was doing for Hara-kiri and added that the pay was good and that I needed the money. He proved not to be such a bad chap after all. He agreed to let me go after I had given him the addresses of the hotels I had still to inspect and the approximate time that I expected to stay at each one.

'There's another thing,' I said, struck by a sudden idea. 'Have you had a complaint from Mr Coberley?'

'A complaint? About what, sir?'

'Well, it seems there must be a gang of louts at work. They could be the arsonists as well, don't you think?'

'As well as what, sir?'

'Somebody smeared grease – butter, he thinks – on the steps outside his house and his wife took a nasty toss and hurt her head. I expect they told you about it at the nursing home.'

'And so, sir?'

'Then comes this burnt-out house. Coberley had an option to purchase it and it got destroyed. Doesn't that seem to add up? It could all be part of a vendetta against the Coberleys.'

'And the murder of Miss Mundy? How do you fit that in?'

'A clear case of a mugging. It wouldn't be the first one which has ended fatally. My theory is that these louts killed the girl after she left here. They must have gone further in mugging her than they had ever intended, or else she fought back and one of them used a knife on her. I imagine he only threatened her with it at first and then lost his head. To me it all adds up. They must have thought the old house was already Mr Coberley's property, so saw a chance of getting rid of the body and avenging themselves on Mr Coberley at one and the same time, even after the greasy steps incident. It looks like a real campaign of hate and revenge to me.'

'Do I understand that you are a writer, sir?' Although his tone was inoffensive, the implication of the words was plain.

'Yes. I told you about the job I am doing for Mr McMaster,' I said evenly.

'Just so, sir. You would need plenty of imagination for literary work, of course.'

'I suppose I might say the same about *your* job,' I retorted.

'True, in a way, sir, but *we* have to establish actual facts before our imagination (which is to say our theorising) is allowed to come into play. You have no facts whatever to support your theories. It is highly unlikely that a gang of louts put grease on Mr Coberley's doorstep. That would be merely a child's thoughtless trick and far more likely to have been carried out by some of his own boys; it is equally unlikely that a gang of young hooligans would have known that Mr Coberley had any interest in the old house. Further to that, we have had no complaints of muggers in this town. Then again, if a gang had stabbed that young woman to death, they wouldn't have risked picking up the body and bringing it on to Mr Wotton's premises. They might have tumbled it over a hedge into somebody's front garden, but after that they would have scarpered, believe you me. Now, sir, is there anything you know – actually *know* – about this business and which you would like to confide to me? You arrived, I understand, before any of the other guests and you are the only one of them who is still here.'

'I don't know a thing which would help you, Inspector, and that's flat. Anyway, you claim that there is no reason to suspect hooliganism, but what about the burnt-out car found blocking the byroad to the old convent just close at hand?'

'The car was left – abandoned, of course – by thieves, sir. It has nothing to do with the Mundy case.'

'That body was never part of the bonfire at the old house, Inspector.'

'The chief fireman's evidence at the inquest would seem to indicate that, sir, but what makes you so certain?'

I decided that I had gone far enough, so I said that I thought it a possibility and said nothing more about Gloria's hair. I added that I thought nets should be cast as wide as possible, that was all. He said that the police always considered a case from every angle and that perhaps I knew very little of the world outside the ivory tower (as he had heard it called) of a novelist. This nettled me. I reminded him that I was also a journalist. I then said, 'Have you ever heard of a sheila-ma-gig, Inspector?'

'I can't say I have, sir.' Having set me down, as he thought, he was good-humoured again. 'Is it a kind of jack-in-the-box?'

'No. You might do worse than study the subject,' I said. 'I think Miss Mundy was a bit of a sheila-ma-gig.'

'You wouldn't care to explain your meaning, sir?'

'No. You are much too young,' I said.

He looked at me, but all he said was: 'Thank you for your help, sir. I had better see Mr Wotton now. Perhaps you would be good enough to locate him for me. I do not want to bring the servants into this part of my enquiry just yet.'

*　　*　　*

Before I left Beeches Lawn the three of us discussed the inspector's visit and revealed to each other what had been said. Whether Anthony and Celia told me *all* that had passed between them and the inspector and whether Anthony had confided fully in Celia and *vice versa*, there was no telling.

'The whole business is complicated because of the accident to Mrs Coberley,' I said at the end of the discussion. 'But for that, I would agree wholeheartedly that the murder was committed deliberately by somebody who detested Gloria or was very much afraid of the harm she could do him or her. That the fire was started deliberately to cover up the identity of the corpse can't possibly be disputed, but I think the burnt-out car explains itself. The old house was a cover-up.'

'Somebody who hated Gloria or was afraid of her? You've got a wide choice there, I fancy,' said Anthony. 'She was a real little pot of poison. Did you know about that Italian artist fellow who committed suicide after he got mixed up with her?'

'You think Rouse ought to cast his net a lot wider than he seems to be doing? That's exactly what I told him.'

'I suppose she did turn up here *unexpectedly*?' said Celia suddenly and with obvious meaning.

'Oh, for goodness' sake!' shouted Anthony. 'Of course she did! And now will you lay off? Do you want to see me doing a thirty-year stretch for killing her? Stop picking on me, for God's sake! I thought we'd done with all that!'

I decided, rightly or wrongly, to speak my mind.

'Look here, you two,' I said, 'if you don't take care, you are going to land one another in the cart if you continue with all this damn silly bickering. Celia, you foolish girl, you must have known, even if he hadn't told you, that you weren't marrying a man unspotted by the world. I can't think what woman would want to marry Sir Galahad. He may have been perfection perfected, but I bet he was the biggest prig on earth and the most blasted, pie-faced boring do-gooder ever to have out-miracled Pollyanna. Why don't you grow up? Your job is to stick by Anthony and back him through thick and thin. Where's that "Voice that breathed o'er Eden" gone to?'

'The voice that breathed o'er Eden was the voice of the serpent,' said Anthony, red in the face. 'Get lost, Corin! Drop dead, if you prefer it! One more crack out of you in criticism of my wife and I'll knock you silly.'

'Oh, Anthony!' said Celia. Before she could add, 'My hero!' I slid out. My bags were already packed. I left without formal leave-taking, reflecting with some self-satisfaction that Dame Beatrice* herself would have been the first to congratulate me on my handling of a domestic situation which, if Celia had been kinder and wiser, need never have arisen between her and Anthony.

I went back to my flat, left some laundry and a note for the woman who 'did' for me, re-packed and telephoned the first of the hotels to let the manager know that I should be along early on the following day. They had all been warned by McMaster that I could give only short notice of my visits, so that nobody could say exactly when these would be. The result was that I had been offered various types of accommodation, from an attic room in the staff quarters to a room in an annexe, to a luxurious suite on the ground floor which happened to be vacant at the time of my arrival. I had accepted what was offered without comment, regarding it as the luck of the draw so far as bedrooms were concerned. The food, drink and other amenities had always been beyond praise, so I had nothing to complain about.

The first of the Cornish hotels had been purchased from an old-established family which could no longer afford to keep it up, even by turning it into a tourist attraction. It was somewhat forbidding from the outward view, a very plain-looking Georgian house whose south façade was relieved from otherwise uncompromising austerity by a very fine pillared portico and the addition on either side of twin pavilions, light, graceful and charming.

I sub-edited the brochure for this house, finding little to add or alter, and telephoned McMaster, with whom I kept in touch when I was ready to pass on to the next hotel. When I handed in my key to the receptionist, she produced a letter for me.

As soon as I scanned the envelope I knew that the writing was unknown to me. As it had been re-addressed from my publishers'

London address, I took it for fan-mail, thrust it into my pocket and did not read it until I was in my room at the second Cornish hotel. This hotel was, as a building, the most interesting and unusual of all those which I had surveyed. It had begun as a monastery, had been fortified later by one of its abbots, had passed into private hands in the sixteenth century; from then onwards it had been altered and enlarged until the company of which McMaster was a director had taken it over, demolished its most grotesque and unfortunate features and left it in the form which might have been the intention of the original planners, at any rate so far as its outward appearance was concerned. Inside, like all the other McMaster hotels I had visited, it was almost boringly luxurious.

The room allotted to me was in one of the flanking-towers. It was small, but it looked straight out to sea and to the left and right there were magnificent views of the south Cornish coast. It was not until I began to undress to take a pre-dinner bath that I thought of the letter. It was from (of all people) Miss Eglantine Brockworth.

'I take it very ill,' the letter ran, 'that you did not come to see me in hospital before you left Beeches Lawn. I have much to say to you and all is strictly confidential, so I can only tell it to someone I can trust. I observed you closely during the short time we were together and noted that you conducted yourself with propriety and self-restraint and this encourages me to confide in you. Come as soon as you can. The rozzers are rounding us all up and time is short.'

After dinner I rang up Beeches Lawn and got Celia.

'I've had a letter from your aunt,' I said, 'sent on by my publishers. She wants me to visit her in hospital, but I hardly know her, so I don't think it's quite my scene.'

'Meaning you hate visiting people in hospital,' said Celia perceptively. 'Well, don't go. She's a cagey old thing. She asked me to lend her that novel of yours. I thought she wanted to read it, but now I can see it was a way of getting in touch with you through your publisher without our knowing what she had in mind.'

'Perhaps I ought to go,' I said. 'It seems unkind not to, now that she's asked me. After all, she's a very old lady.'

'Please yourself, Corin, but I ought to warn you that they hate her at the hospital and it spills over on to her visitors. I go to see her from a sense of duty, but you don't have to bother.'

'I'll write to her, then,' I said, 'and tell her that I'm quite tied up at present, but I'll visit her as soon as I can.'

9
Chaucer's Prioress

I was so well up to time that I decided to go and see Aunt Eglantine before I tackled the hotel in Dorset. As that was my last assignment I thought I could expect VIP treatment in the matter of a room so long as I let the manager know, some days beforehand, that he was to expect me. I felt that it was only civil to let Celia know when I proposed to visit her aunt, so I telephoned and asked when the visiting hours were. She replied with cordiality and a warmth which surprised me and invited me to lunch with them, as hospital visits were restricted to the early evenings except for patients on open order.

'And you must come back for dinner and the night,' she said. 'Longer, if you can spare the time.'

'How about Anthony?' I asked. She understood me and replied that Anthony would also look forward to seeing me again.

'We both took your words very much to heart,' she said. 'It was good of you to speak out the way you did. We were making fools of ourselves, but it's perfectly all right now.'

'Is Rouse bothering you again?'

'Not for more than a week now; in fact he has only called on us once since you left and that was to ask Anthony whether he was sure he had identified the corpse correctly. We thought it was a very odd question, but, of course, in a police investigation I suppose there has to be no doubt about whose death is being looked into. From what I hear, he's now busy harassing all the people who were staying or had stayed here at what he calls "the crucial time". Anyway, we'll tell you all about it when we see you. When will that be?'

'Would a week from now be all right?'

I put in another couple of nights at the hotel in Cornwall, completed my amendments to the two Cornish brochures and sent them off to McMaster with a note to tell him that I was on the last lap of my course. Then I went back to my flat for another change of clothes and to deal with a crop of correspondence and stayed there until I went again to Beeches Lawn.

There was no doubt about the genuineness of Anthony's welcome and Celia kissed me when I arrived, which was very pleasant. By what appeared to be mutual agreement, although it was unspoken, we avoided any reference to Gloria Mundy or Detective-Inspector Rouse and, after a lazy afternoon terminated by a cup of tea, Anthony drove me to the hospital, which was not in the town, and took me up to Aunt Eglantine's room.

'I don't want *you*,' she said to him. 'Come back for this young man in an hour's time.'

'I'm glad you've got a room to yourself,' I said, when Anthony had left us.

'The nurses aren't,' she said, her plump, purple-veined old face creasing into an impish gleam of amusement. 'I keep 'em on their toes, you know. Well, what have you come to see me about?'

'I thought you had called me to your side by white witchcraft, dear Madame Eglantine,' I said.

'Ah,' she said, looking pleased, 'you remembered that I am named for Chaucer, not Shakespeare.'

'Yes, but Shakespeare's "sweet musk roses" seem to partner you well enough.'

She gave a girlish little giggle.

'I suspect flattery,' she said. 'You just behave yourself. Are you surprised to find that I am not under arrest?'

'But you didn't kill Gloria Mundy, did you?' The words slipped out involuntarily, but I could not recall them. However, she received them with great good humour.

'I thought of it,' she said, 'but I decided she wasn't worth a life sentence – not that it would have lasted very long in my case. I give myself about another five years of life, that's all. The law is very unjust

78

in certain respects. They would have awarded me thirty years, I suppose, but I should have slipped out of their hands in five, whereas a boy of twenty, even with a remission for good conduct, would not have got away with that, would he? Did they show you the body?'

'Yes, Anthony and I both saw it.'

'I read about the inquest in the papers. They said that nothing but the hair was recognisable. Is that so?'

'Well, yes. Still, it made identification a very simple matter.'

'That hair was a wig, of course. It was two-coloured to create an effect.'

'It was not a wig.'

'How do you know?'

'Naming no names, I know a man who used to wash her hair for her.'

'She bore Anthony a child. Did you know that?'

'Dear Madame Eglantine, you are romancing.'

'No,' she said, 'it is quite true. I know. I listen behind doors, you see.'

'You are a disgraceful old party, then.'

'Oh,' she said, 'listening behind doors is an art.'

'No, it isn't. You mean a craft. That's where the word 'crafty' comes from. Originally it was used to describe people who listened behind doors.'

'You are making that up. Anyhow, it is an art, and one not unlike your own. You invent stories and so do I. I invent them for when the door opens suddenly and I am caught out. Well, what have you been doing with yourself since I saw you last? Nothing very creditable, I'll be bound.'

'You tell me about Gloria's baby and then I'll tell you all about my wicked deeds. What did you get hold of when you listened behind doors?'

'You first,' she said; so I described the two Cornish hotels and added a couple of stories straight out of Rabelais concerning my doings in each. She laughed and laughed.

'I must tell the nurses,' she said. 'It will keep them happy for weeks.'

'I expect they've heard better ones from the young doctors,' I said. 'Now it's your turn.'

'Why haven't you married, personable young man?'

'No money to get married on at the time, and now I've let the chance go by.'

'Nonsense. I prophesy that you will meet her again before long. Are you any good at picking up stitches?'

'No, nor threads. Come on, play fair.'

'Oh, yes, you want to know what I heard. First, that girl did not turn up out of the blue.'

'She didn't?'

'No. Anthony Wotton asked her to come.'

'You've got the story wrong.'

'I never get stories wrong.' I thought of Rubens and the portrait in the old house and said nothing. Encouraged or else irritated by my silence, she went on, 'She came to blackmail him on the strength of the baby.'

I said sternly, 'You really must not tell these awful whoppers, Madame Eglantine.'

'Chaucer spelt it with an "e" and a "y", whereas my misguided parents preferred Shakespeare's rendering. What kind of flower is eglantine? Did your teachers tell you that?'

'Eglantine is the old word for the sweetbrier. That's why Oberon connected it with musk roses, I suppose,' I told her.

'I must remember to spell it Shakespeare's way in my will. I shall leave you a competence. I am a very wealthy woman. Write both spellings down for me. Underline the one and run a light stroke neatly through the other.'

I took up the writing-pad which was on her bedside locker and printed in my best capitals EGLENTYNE and EGLANTINE.'

'Which is to be underlined and which is to have a line drawn through it?' I asked.

'Don't ask stupid questions!' she snapped at me. I drew a faint line through the first name and underlined more thickly the other. I deduced that she was getting tired, so I rose to go. She was having none of that, and ordered me to sit down again. She drew the writing-pad towards her and smiled.

'I shall never get out of here alive, you know,' she said. 'They are witches and they meet at Hetty Pegler's Tump.'

'I've been there,' I said, anxious to avoid the discussion of the *Malleus Maleficarum* which seemed imminent, 'but I didn't crawl inside.'

'The Neoliths must have lacked stature,' said Aunt Eglantine. 'Did you ever visit Grime's Graves?'

This subject lasted us for the remainder of my visit. A warning bell sounded and a nurse came in and told me that visiting hours were up. I bent over and kissed Aunt Eglantine.

'You must come again,' she said, 'before they finish me off.'

I left the hospital and crossed the road to where Anthony had parked the car. He lowered the book he was reading and then tossed it on to the back seat.

'Well,' he said, 'you stayed a lot longer than I thought you would.'

'I did make one attempt to leave because I thought I was tiring her, but she wouldn't have it. I suppose she gets bloody bored in there.'

'Did she mention Gloria?'

'Yes. She told me two things about her, both of them sheer invention, I feel sure.'

'Did she get on to the *Malleus*?'

'No. Hetty Pegler intervened and we also talked about Grime's Graves.'

He started the engine. I stared out through the windscreen and hoped he would not ask what Aunt Eglantine had said about Gloria's hair and her child, not that I believed either story. When the remark came, it was not a question but a simple assertion.

'She has a bee in her bonnet about my having given Gloria a child,' he said. 'Sooner or later she tells everybody so. I suppose you got it, too.'

'Yes, she did rather throw the information at me. I took it for what it was worth – sheer balderdash.'

To my astonishment he said he would tell me the truth, as he might need the help of a true friend later on. I realised, not for the first time, that he was desperately afraid of what Detective-Inspector Rouse might ferret out concerning his former relationship with Gloria and I realised, too, that he was far more concerned with the effect which possible revelations would have on his marriage than fears for his own personal safety.

The last thing on earth that I wanted was to become any more deeply involved in his affairs than I already was, but *noblesse oblige*, as, in its blackmailing way, it usually does, so I said something trite about doing anything I could. There was a long silence until I remarked that surely we were going rather a long way round to get back to Beeches Lawn.

'Oh, Celia won't be expecting us just yet,' he said. 'I told her you would probably need a pick-me-up in a pub after spending an hour solo with Aunt Eglantine. Anyway, I was going to tell you about the baby.'

'Good Lord! So the story was true! I thought she was making it up because she dislikes you,' I said.

'She doesn't dislike me personally. She simply thinks that I'm not good enough for Celia. That may be so, but Celia accepted me of her own free will, so our marriage is our business and not the business of that frustrated old demonologist.'

'Did you know Aunt Eglantine before your marriage?'

'No, thank goodness. She had to be invited to the wedding, but that was the first time I had met her.'

'She told me some cock and bull story – '

'About that baby? It wasn't mine, of course, and, to give you some idea of what Gloria was like, I must tell you the whole story. It happened while I was still having this damn silly affair with her and, of course, before I began to rumble her. She had this friend who had got herself mixed up with some extraordinary sect in America and desperately wanted to free herself from them and come to England. The scheme was for me to take Gloria to meet her at the airport and motor them both back to Gloria's flat.

'I couldn't see any harm in that, so I did it. The friend turned out to be a waif-like creature with (what had not been told me, although I don't suppose it would have made any difference at the time I agreed to meet her) a two-month-old baby. Well, now, Corin, the next bit is a blur in my memory, but when we got to the car I found the baby dumped in my arms, Gloria with an arm over my shoulders and the skinny Lizzie taking the photograph, complete with giggles.'

'What photograph?'

'My photograph holding the baby, of course, with Gloria's arm round both of us and the two girls laughing their heads off. I took it as a joke at the time, fool that I was.'

'Sounds like the makings of a promising farce,' I said. 'Stock situation, what?'

'May sound like that to you, but to me it's been a nightmare. I've lived on the edge of a volcano these last years, and when she turned up here I was scared out of my wits and I'll tell you this, old man: I never had a better moment in my life than when we both identified that dead girl as Gloria Mundy. What other rubbish did old Eg hand out to you?'

'That Gloria's red and black hair was a wig.'

We covered the miles between the hospital and the house before we spoke again. He turned in at the lane which led up to his garage, parked the car, locked the shed behind us and then, as we walked through the kitchen garden, I said, 'That puzzles me, you know. It was the only thing we had to go by in recognising Gloria. Why wasn't it destroyed in the fire along with the rest of her?'

'I would rather not think about it. That awful body is something I want to forget.'

'Yes, I know. Strange, though, that Miss Brockworth should have made such a remark.'

'Very strange,' he agreed. 'Please don't let Celia pump you too much about the visit to the hospital. She's a devil at worming things out of people. I convinced her long ago that there was nothing but the mildest of shipboard flirtations between Gloria and me – at least, I thought I had – but Gloria's death has stirred up old doubts in

Celia's heart, so, for my sake, watch your step, if you don't mind, old man.'

'Fear nothing,' I said. 'You are walking beside the man who lied himself black in the face to the magistrates in Pontyprydd after that rugger match. Remember?'

'Vaguely.'

'Oh, come on now! Don't you realise that I sacrificed my immortal soul on your behalf on that auspicious occasion?'

'Oh, well, thanks,' he said, and we were both cheerful when Celia herself opened the door to us.

'So Aunt Eglantine didn't treat you to a dissertation on the *Malleus*, or you wouldn't be so happy,' she said. 'Marigold Coberley's here, but she won't stay for dinner.'

Marigold was sitting in an armchair by the fire and looked lost in that huge drawing-room. I was relieved to note that there was no trace of her tumble down the butterslide steps. Her face was quite unmarked and she was as beautiful as ever. Evidently, there had been no need for plastic surgery. All the same, there was something very wrong somewhere, for I could see that she had been crying. I took her hand, not to shake it but because I wanted, suddenly and urgently, to have some physical contact with her. Her fingers gripped mine and I knew that she understood the sympathy I did not express in words. She said, 'The police have arrested my husband, Corin. What am I going to do?'

'What? Why on earth arrest Cranford?' demanded Anthony, as Marigold released my hand and huddled into the armchair with her fists pressed against her eyes.

It was Celia who answered. 'Rouse or somebody else at the police station has had a letter,' she explained. 'It was anonymous and in the ordinary way they might not have taken it so seriously as they have done, although, of course, they do get anonymous tip-offs which have to be investigated. Unfortunately what was in the letter only confirmed Rouse's own suspicions. The police think they have found the murder weapon, and it points straight at Cranford. That, and Marigold's accident, have convinced them.'

'So what was in the letter?' I asked.

'The writer claimed to have seen a young woman with red and black hair kneeling on the schoolhouse steps. The inference that she was responsible for Marigold's accident was too obvious to be ignored.'

'So what was that about the murder weapon?' asked Anthony.

'That's the devastating part of it. When the police sifted through all the ashes and rubble of the burnt-out old house they found the remains of a long dagger. Of course, at the time they could not connect it with anybody and the fact that they had found it they kept a closely guarded secret until they could trace the owner. When they received this anonymous letter they showed the dagger to Cranford and Marigold.'

'And Cranford recognised it and said so,' said Marigold, looking up and speaking with intensity and with no hint of further tears. 'He told them that he had impounded it from one of the boys and had put it with other bits and pieces that the boys had collected. The various things were in a wooden crate in the old house. He would never have admitted that he recognised the dagger if he had used it to kill that girl, would he? I should have thought that would establish his innocence, if anything could.'

'Did they know he had the key to the old house?' I asked.

'Yes, they did,' said Anthony, 'but that couldn't really have told against him because there was the broken window at the back.'

'So all they have to go on is his own admission that he recognised the dagger.'

'Well, not quite,' said Marigold. I waited, but she added nothing further. Celia renewed an offer which she had made before our return from the hospital, but Marigold refused to stay for dinner and left. Anthony saw her home. When he came back he said that here was a pretty kettle of fish.

'It will absolutely ruin the school,' he went on. 'Even if Cranford is acquitted, nobody is going to leave a boy at a school where the headmaster has been had up on a charge of murder and arson.'

'What do you suppose Mrs Coberley meant when she said that the dagger was not quite the only thing the police had to go on?' I asked.

'I think I know what she meant,' said Anthony. 'Do you remember my telling you what a tiger Coberley can be when anything happens to upset him in connection with Marigold? Well, this won't be the first time he has seen the inside of a gaol. When she herself was acquitted of murder, an acquaintance of his wrote an insulting and vitriolic letter, and Coberley went round and half killed the chap. Coberley had a good lawyer and received a light sentence on a plea of diminished responsibility owing to unreasonable provocation and insupportable emotional stress. The letter was produced in court, but the journalists were told that it was not to appear in their reports of the trial because of the damage it would do to Marigold, who, after all, had been acquitted of the murder she had been charged with.'

'I wonder how he managed to start a school with a charge of grievous bodily harm against him,' I said.

'Oh, he changed his name, of course.'

'How do you know that?'

'Oh, it's wonderful what you hear when an ordinarily abstemious man gets enough of the right stuff sloshing about inside him. One thing – I'm sure he has no idea that he told me the tale.'

'Do you think he killed Gloria Mundy?'

'I don't know. I wonder who it was who tipped him off that it was she who buttered the steps and then called out to Marigold?'

'One of the servants at the school, I guess.'

I stayed the night. The next day I went to my Dorset hotel to begin work on the last of the brochures. Exactly a week later I sent the rest of my notes and alterations to Hara-kiri and went to see Aunt Eglantine again. At Anthony's house I had told him and Celia, over dinner, of the old lady's boast that she was a wealthy woman and of her statement that I was to benefit under her will.

'Of course she isn't wealthy,' Celia had said, 'but it would be quite likely that she had taken a fancy to you and decided to put you in her will.'

'Great expectations!' I said, laughing. So it was with no avaricious intentions that I went to see Aunt Eglantine again.

'It's been a long time,' she said.

86

'Only a week, and I have been very busy.'

'I see they've arrested that sour man who has the beautiful wife. The police must be fools if they think he did it. Will you do something for me?'

'With pleasure, if it is in my power.'

'Get that Bradley woman on to it. She'll sort it out in no time.'

'Dame Beatrice?'

'Who else? Nothing will come of nothing and Gloria Mundy murdered Gloria Mundy. You tell her that. What are you to tell her?'

'That nothing will come of nothing and that Gloria Mundy murdered Gloria Mundy.'

'Swear that you will repeat those words to her. Even *she* cannot make bricks without straw. And don't forget that burnt-out car. Celia told me about it when she came to visit me. Swear?'

'I swear. And now stop exciting yourself. Think of your namesake.'

'What about her?'

> ' "And sikerly she was of greet disport
> And ful plesáunt and amyable of port,
> And peyned hire to countrefete chere
> Of court" '

I quoted solemnly.

'Don't understand a word of it,' she said.

'Sikerly, surely, or certainly; disport, cheerfulness; port, bearing or manner; chere, another word for manner. So now what don't you understand?'

'Why you've come to see me again.'

'If you are thinking of leaving me a million pounds, or whatever it is, I thought I had better keep in with you.'

'Have you remembered what you are to say to Bradley?'

'To Dame Beatrice, yes, but I'll write it down, if you like.'

'Yes, do that,' she said. 'She'll know what I mean. We are twin souls, like Kramer and Sprenger.'

The *Malleus* lasted us for the rest of my visit.

10
Colloquies

I rang to ask Anthony for Dame Beatrice's address and telephone number and then I rang up her secretary and asked for an appointment. I said that I had met Dame Beatrice at Beeches Lawn and had been at the house when murder and arson were committed. Two days later I was at the Stone House on the edge of the New Forest and in conference with the eminent lady.

'So the police have arrested the headmaster,' she said. 'I wonder why?'

I gave her the reasons, so far as I knew them and she nodded as I put to her the various points. When I had finished she sent me out to walk in the forest while she mulled them over. In the hall I encountered a tall, well-proportioned woman who asked why I was leaving so soon. I explained that I had been sent off while Dame Beatrice meditated and asked whether I might borrow one of the walking-sticks which I saw in the umbrella stand, as it helped my thinking to whack at heaps of fallen leaves and stinging-nettles and suchlike extravagances of nature when I was out in the country and in a quandary.

'Help yourself,' she said. 'You might take the dogs out as well. George wants to clean the car and I've got a raft of correspondence to go through, so it would save us both a job if you would do it.'

'So you are the voice on the telephone,' I said.

'And you are the scribe, but not, I hope, the Pharisee, as my esteemed boss would say. You're staying for lunch, then, as we had hoped. There will be another guest, and Dame B. says you are already acquainted with him.'

'Not McMaster?'

'No. This is a man – youngish, I gather – named William Underedge. He represented her at the inquest.'

'So that was it! I wondered why he was there. I thought it must have been because his fiancée, Mrs Wotton's niece, sent him along.'

'No. When Dame B. read about your Beeches Lawn murder and the fire and all the rest of it, she thought it was very interesting. She said she had met a very capable and reliable young man at Mr Wotton's house and bade me page him. I tracked him down, beginning with the London telephone directory and, needing to go no further, got in touch and issued him his marching orders. Apparently, like all people of taste and discernment, he had taken a great fancy to Dame B., short though their acquaintance had been, and he agreed to drop everything and go straight down to Hilcombury, which he knows well because his father used to own a woollen mill down there, and attend the inquest.'

'I shall look forward to meeting him again,' I said politely.

'That will be Underedge now. What a bit of luck! You can take him out with you and give him the story. Dame B. won't want to be bothered with him if she's mulling over whatever news you've brought with you.'

She was not the type to ask what this news was, but, when William Underedge had been admitted, I told both of them that Coberley had been arrested. William Underedge said, 'What absolute nonsense!'

Laura Gavin said that she supposed the police had something to go on, so I told her about the long dagger which had been found among the ashes of the fire.

'But headmasters of prep schools don't go about sticking daggers into people,' she said. 'It's out of character.'

'He wasn't always a headmaster,' said William. 'He was a wealthy businessman before his marriage. My father had some dealings with him when we owned the mill. He was shrewd and perhaps a bit hard, but as straight as they come.'

'Did you ever come up against his bad temper?' I asked.

'Certainly not. I'll tell you another thing.'

'Tell it to Mr Stratford while you're out for your walk,' said Laura. 'I've got a lot to do before lunch. See you later.'

So William and I collected the dogs and took the forest walk to a little bridge over the stream and, as we leant on the rail and looked down at the clear brown water, he said, 'I don't see how they can hold Coberley on the evidence they've got. It isn't really evidence at all.'

'Oh, I don't know. His previous record? The injury to his beautiful wife? His admission that the dagger belonged to him – well, to one of his boys from whom he had impounded it? The fact that he had a key to the old house?'

'Yes, granted, but there is the man himself. Cranford Coberley, so-called, although not the name my father and I knew him by, might conceivably kill a *man* in a fit of passion – it was easy to see that he idolised his wife – but I cannot believe that he would kill a *woman*, certainly not by stabbing her in the back. I thought the medical evidence given at the inquest was very interesting. That stab in the back was probably a woman's crime.'

'Well, it couldn't have been done by Marigold Coberley. She was in the nursing home,' I said. William straightened up and we finished crossing the bridge and whistled up the dogs who had gone chasing off after rabbits. 'She would have been suffering from concussion and severe bruising.'

'I don't know so much,' he argued. 'I gathered that the time of death was very uncertain owing to the extensive burning of the body. The girl could have been killed *before* Mrs Coberley had her accident and, if she was, the whole case against Coberley goes down the drain. As soon as he is brought before the magistrates he will be released. I'm sure of it.'

'Well, for his sake I hope you're right,' I said, 'but that dagger will take some explaining. Nobody but Coberley would have known of its existence in that wooden box in the old house.'

'I bet every boy in the school knew about it. I bet lots of them had handled it before it was impounded. The staff would have known of it, and I daresay the servants too. The person who sold or gave it to the boy would have known of it. The police need to cast their net a lot wider than poor Coberley. I expect they are being pressurised and think that any arrest is better than none. Incidentally, how do you come into the affair? In other words, why are you here?'

'I am Miss Eglantine Brockworth's emissary to Dame Beatrice.'

'Miss Brockworth isn't as crazy as people think.'

'I don't know about that. I am to make a cryptic statement to Dame Beatrice.'

'A quotation from that ancient tract she's so fond of?'

'I don't think so. I am to tell Dame Beatrice that nothing will come of nothing.'

'I wouldn't call that a cryptic statement. I would call it a self-evident axiom.'

'Ah, but that's only half of it. The other half is to the effect that Gloria killed Gloria.'

'I don't see anything mysterious about that, either. People who get themselves murdered are often responsible for what happens to them. Think of the silly girls who thumb lifts. Think of impossible wives murdered by husbands who've come to the end of their tether and battered wives who can't see any way out of their miseries except the death of the person responsible for them.'

'Those are not the only reasons for murder.'

'Granted. As for Miss Mundy, I did not see enough of her to judge whether she could be a possible murderee, but she struck me as being an unpleasant type of girl. What did you make of her?'

'Like you, not much, but I don't think I would have cared about cultivating her acquaintance.'

We turned back at the end of half an hour. During our return stroll we dropped the subject of Gloria Mundy and talked about the forest itself, its ponies, the gypsies, the rights and duties of the Verderers, the privileges granted to the commoners, the deer, the care of the trees, and on all these topics I found William Underedge far better informed than I was.

He stayed for lunch and when he had gone, Dame Beatrice, Mrs Gavin and I settled down, so to speak, and I passed on Miss Brockworth's message. Dame Beatrice took it more seriously than I had anticipated.

'She said that, did she? Interesting,' was her comment.

'I suppose what the Delphic oracle said was interesting to those who could make head or tail of it,' said Laura Gavin.

'Oh, I think Miss Brockworth's statements had a very plain and straightforward meaning. I wonder whether it was guesswork on her part, or whether she has anything definite to go on? You would not know, of course, any more than I do, Mr Stratford. So the police have arrested Mr Coberley? How very precipitate of them. Well, now, is there anything you can add to what you have already told me?'

'I don't think so, Dame Beatrice. You mentioned guesswork. Don't you think that's all it was, and some of it rather malicious?'

'Her niece may have told her about Mr Wotton's premarital acquaintanceship with Miss Mundy. Incidentally, but for your information, when I had my talks with her, I asked her to write down some sentences which I dictated. They contained a disproportionate number of a's, o's, d's, g's, p's and q's.'

'I think I see what you were getting at. My guess is that she carefully joined up the rounded tops of those letters, instead of leaving them partly open, as many people do when they are writing fairly fast.'

'Exactly. Miss Brockworth dislikes leaving unnecessary gaps.'

'So what she doesn't know, she invents.'

'Her deductions are logical, and, despite what may appear to be evidence to the contrary, she is shrewd, precise and well-informed.'

'Her information is acquired by listening behind doors,' I said. 'She may have heard Gloria trying to blackmail Anthony.'

I told the story of Gloria and the young mother from America, and the baby dumped into the arms of the unsuspecting Anthony. I told of the photograph of him and Gloria in the guise of fond parents. When I had finished she cackled and made a comment I did not want to hear, but of which I could hardly deny the significance.

'She had forged a powerful weapon,' she said, 'if Mr Wotton has a jealous wife.'

'Yes,' I said. 'If the whole truth came out, there could be as strong a case against Wotton as against Coberley. Then there is McMaster, who also had an affair with the girl. There may be others. What if the wretched Gloria got money by blackmail and one of her other victims, not Wotton or McMaster, tracked her down and killed her?'

'Blackmail comes under the heading of dangerous trades, certainly. Not only is it a major crime, but the blackmailer can never be certain that one day one of the victims will not turn, like the proverbial worm. "Publish and be damned" is not only a courageous but the most sensible reply to blackmailers. If it came to the point, they would hardly dare to carry out their threats.'

'Look,' I said, 'I don't know whether Coberley killed Gloria or not, but I don't want to see Wotton or McMaster in the dock in his place.'

' "Why, gentle sweet, you shall see no such thing",' said Laura Gavin mockingly, and Dame Beatrice added, 'Ring up Mrs Wotton and ask her to find out whether Mrs Coberley would care for me to call on her. I have my own reasons for believing in Mr Coberley's technical innocence.'

'His *technical* innocence?'

'Oh, I think it more than likely that Mr Coberley might have killed Miss Mundy, if – '

'If somebody else hadn't beaten him to it,' said Laura Gavin. I returned to Beeches Lawn puzzled and perturbed.

To my astonishment, Marigold Coberley's response to Celia's call (which was in person and not over the telephone) was a blunt and apparently unalterable refusal to entertain a visit from Dame Beatrice.

'But how extremely foolish of her,' I said. 'Surely she knows of the immense reputation Dame Beatrice has built up for herself? Surely she knows of her standing at the Home Office? Surely she realises that Dame Beatrice would not offer help if she didn't believe that poor old Coberley is innocent of the charge? Can't you tackle the silly girl again and persuade her to have a bit of sense?'

'No, I can't. I can't say more to her than I have said already. Have a go at her yourself, Corin, if you think you can do any better than I've done. I've talked my head off and done no good at all. She must be mad to refuse such wonderful help, but there it is. She says it's up to the lawyers. It's their job now.'

With some embarrassment I informed Dame Beatrice of the result of my telephone call. She listened to my apologetic explanation that Marigold must be suffering from severe shock and depression and did not attempt to cut me short. At the end she said, 'You have told me what I expected to hear.'

'That Marigold Coberley would turn down your most kind and generous offer?'

'Yes. Come and see me again, if you can spare the time.'

'Right away,' I said. When I arrived I repeated my question: did she know that Marigold would refuse her help?

'Not exactly that. What you have told me confirms my view that Marigold Coberley believes that her husband *did* kill Gloria Mundy. Oh, well, if the cup is full, perhaps the saucer will be more receptive. I shall go to visit Cranford Coberley himself.'

'If it's a permitted question,' I said diffidently, 'do you believe that Coberley is innocent?'

'Well,' she said, 'the time sequence may well be wrong.'

'Oh? In what way?' I enquired.

'I think I agree with William Underedge's theory that the murder may have been committed before Mrs Coberley slipped on the school-house steps and hurt herself.'

'If that could be proved, it would go a long way towards removing Coberley's motive for murder,' I said.

'Yes,' agreed Dame Beatrice, 'if it could be proved, but that proof may be difficult to find and it may be non-existent. I will hear what the man himself has to say. I doubt whether *he* will refuse to see me, although he would be within his rights to do so.'

'He would be a fool to refuse help,' said Laura. 'As for his wife, even if she does think him guilty, surely she wants to do the best she can for him.'

'Possibly she thinks she *is* doing the best she can for him,' said Dame Beatrice. 'She may have heard that I have a passion for finding out the truth, so, if she really believes that he murdered Miss Mundy, she will do everything she can to keep him out of my clutches. Well, now, Mr Stratford, I need to know the address of the hospital. I shall look in on Miss Brockworth tomorrow morning at eleven. Would it fit in with your plans to meet me at the hospital gates at twelve?'

'But they won't let you in at eleven,' I said. 'The visiting hours, you know.'

She grinned at me with a mirthless stretching of her mouth. Laura Gavin told me impatiently not to be silly.

'There isn't a hospital in the land which would keep Dame Beatrice out,' she said. I apologised. Dame Beatrice cackled and our next meeting was arranged forthwith. I parked in the hospital grounds at a quarter to twelve to make certain that I did not keep Dame Beatrice waiting, got out of my car to stretch my legs after having driven to the hospital from McMaster's Dorset hotel where I had spent the night, and saw Laura Gavin at the wheel of another car. I went up to it and she wound down the window.

'Good morning,' I said. 'I've been wondering why Dame Beatrice asked me to meet her here.'

'I think she wants to tell you what she and Miss Brockworth have had to say to one another. Are you free for the rest of the day?'

At this moment Dame Beatrice emerged from the main door of the hospital. She was accompanied by nurses who were attending her as though she were royalty. I walked towards them and Dame Beatrice took her leave. I escorted her to her car.

'We are all to lunch at Beeches Lawn,' she said. 'Will you lead the way and then Laura can follow you.'

It was clear that Anthony and Celia welcomed us with relief as well as with enthusiasm. Celia, in fact, went so far as to say that poor Cranford Coberley would be all right now.

'Not necessarily,' Dame Beatrice said. 'So much depends upon when the murder was committed. Unless that can be established – and upon present evidence it looks almost impossible to say when the killing took place – it is the vexed question of an alibi which faces us. This afternoon I shall hear all that Mr Coberley can tell me about his movements after the last time that Miss Mundy was seen at the old house.'

'The worst of it is,' said Anthony, 'that people living their ordinary lives and carrying out their normal duties have no idea that they may need to provide themselves with an alibi for any particular time. I doubt very much whether I could remember what I was doing or where I was at any particular time between when Gloria rushed out of this house in a blazing temper because of naughty old Eg and the soup, and the time the body was discovered after the fire.'

Over lunch the three of us, Anthony, Celia and myself, filled in the blanks to the best of our ability. After lunch Dame Beatrice went over the various points and Laura Gavin took down our answers. It did not seem to me that these helped very much. She had a complete list of the people who had been at lunch on the day that Gloria had shown up, and I had already told her of the visit paid by McMaster and how he had had to stay the night because of the storm, and we mentioned the departure and return of Kay Shortwood and Roland Thornbury on the same day.

'They saw Gloria at the window of the old house, so she was certainly alive then,' said Celia, 'and Aunt Eglantine saw her after that.'

'So that narrows the time a bit,' said Anthony. 'Aunt Eg met her at the old house when she elected to climb that rotten staircase and brought it down with her.'

'She told me about that,' said Dame Beatrice. 'It seems that she wanted to look at a valuable picture which was kept in the old house.' She looked enquiringly at Anthony and added, 'It seems a curious place to have kept it, if it really was valuable.'

'Oh, my aunt got it into her head that it was a Rubens, but, of course, it was nothing of the sort. It was by an unknown artist and I shouldn't think it was worth more than a few pounds.'

'It was a striking bit of painting, though,' I said. 'I saw it when Coberley took me into the old house. It could have been a portrait of Gloria herself, as a matter of fact.'

'So Anthony told me when he first came clean about his association with Gloria before we were married,' said Celia.

'So you refused to have it in this house, I suppose,' said Laura Gavin.

'No. It had always hung in the old house,' said Anthony. 'My father would not have it in here.' He told the story of his great-grandfather and the original of the portrait. 'I imagine the woman had a child by the old reprobate,' he concluded, 'and Gloria was her direct descendant. To that extent I suppose she can claim – as she did – to be a distant relative of mine.'

'What form did the portrait take?' asked Dame Beatrice. 'Was it a portrait-bust, a full-length study, or what? Was it in the clothes of the period, and, if so, what would that period have been? Miss Brockworth could not describe the portrait to me, as she said she had never seen it.'

'We took care she didn't see it,' said Celia. 'It was a reclining nude and, although the girl was so thin, there was a sort of horrible suggestiveness about it which was – well, would have been to anybody of my aunt's generation – quite revolting.'

'Oh, nonsense!' said Anthony. Celia opened her mouth, but caught my eye and said nothing. Dame Beatrice asked what, to me, was a surprising question.

'I know from William Underedge, who kindly attended the inquest for me, that you and Mr Stratford were called upon to identify the body,' she said to Anthony, 'and that it was the parti-coloured hair alone which aided you. Would you, Mr Wotton, have been equally sure of your identification if you had been shown the whole body of the deceased?'

Considering what, presumably, had been Anthony's previous relationship with Gloria, I thought this was an outrageous question. Anthony did not look at Celia, but he answered Dame Beatrice steadily and seriously enough.

'I don't see what difference it would have made,' he said, 'because I suppose the body wouldn't have been recognisable, either by me or by anybody else, if it had been burnt as badly as the face was burnt.'

Dame Beatrice turned to me.

'Mr Stratford, from what you have told me, I gather that you were the first person to see Miss Mundy arrive at Beeches Lawn.'

I looked out of the window at the trees and shrubs which bisected the garden and, turning again to Dame Beatrice, I agreed and added,

'She came along the front of the house, where we are now. I saw her from my bedroom window.'

'So much I remember. She came in from the direction of the playing-field. To do that, would she have had to pass a convent which was mentioned to me in connection with quite another matter?'

'It's no longer a convent,' said Celia. 'You are talking about that car which was burnt up?'

'And Miss Mundy arrived here on the Sunday I left?' went on Dame Beatrice.

'On the Sunday, yes. Some local craftsmen use the building now, but they wouldn't have seen Gloria go past the place,' said Anthony. 'The old convent is empty at weekends.'

'Splendid,' said Dame Beatrice. I thought I knew the reason for her satisfaction. All the same, I wondered how Gloria could have known that the convent building would have been deserted on the Sunday of her arrival. Dame Beatrice, who appeared to be able to read my mind without asking questions of me, said calmly, 'She asked what the building was, I suppose, and one of the local people or perhaps one of the schoolboys told her.'

'I wonder whether she saw that burnt-out car,' said Celia. 'I don't think the police knew about it until the lessee of the convent building reported it, though. It probably wasn't there when Gloria came that way.'

'I do not see how it could have been,' said Dame Beatrice. 'Does your gardener work on Sundays?'

'Certainly not. I'm a churchwarden,' said Anthony, 'and am in honour bound to keep the fourth Commandment.'

'Except in the case of cook and her scullery maid,' said Celia. 'There are limits to his pious observance of the Sabbath. He does love his midday Sunday dinner, although we do have a cold meal at night.'

11
A Conference with the Accused

The next question was put to me personally. Dame Beatrice asked me whether I wrote shorthand, adding that as, among my other activities, I was a newspaper reporter (or so William Underedge had told her), no doubt I numbered shorthand among my accomplishments. Wondering what this was leading up to, I admitted that this was so.

'Good,' she said. 'You shall accompany me upon my mission.'

'And we hope,' said Laura Gavin, 'that shades of the prison-house will not begin to close upon the growing boy.'

'You mean you want me to sit in on your interview with Coberley?' I said. 'He won't like that very much.'

'Did you not get on well with him when you met?'

'Oh, I saw very little of him, but he did show me over the old house one morning.'

'Well, he can refuse to talk to me in front of you, but I think he would prefer you to Laura. He may even feel he has a friend at court when he sees you with me.'

So off we went. Apparently she had made all the arrangements beforehand, for we were taken straightaway to the governor's office, where Dame Beatrice was received with deference.

'You had better see Coberley in here,' said the governor and he sent off the prison officer who had brought us into his presence to conduct Coberley to the sanctum. 'I told him that we were expecting a visit from you and that he could have his lawyer present at the interview if he so wished, but he said that he had met you and needed no other help.'

Coberley looked better than I had expected. He was well-shaven and was wearing a good suit. His demeanour was cheerful. In fact, he looked fresher and more alive than he had appeared at Beeches Lawn. I think he had shed the image of the headmaster and had reverted to that of the business tycoon who, no doubt, had been in tight places before and had come out of them unscathed. He greeted us with an impartial, 'Very good of you both to come,' shook hands with us and the governor, and then the prison officer left us and we, so to speak, settled down, myself at the desk ready to take notes, the other two in chairs adjacent to one another.

'I take it that you know the magistrates have decided I must stand trial,' said Coberley. 'It means the end of the school, so far as I am concerned, of course, but my first assistant will carry on and if the boys stay he will buy me out and take over completely. That is all arranged. Whatever the result of the trial, I can hardly go back there myself. I shall miss the boys, of course, but Marigold will enjoy living in our villa in the south of France. I am pretty sure I shall be able to join her there. I don't see how this charge can possibly stick. There isn't enough evidence against me to hang a dog.'

'A pity the magistrates did not share that view,' said Dame Beatrice drily.

'Oh, the Bench always believe the yarns the police cook up,' said Coberley, appearing less and less like my previous picture of him. 'The Chief Constable brought pressure to bear on that rather obtuse detective-inspector, I think, so an arrest had to be made and I drew the short straw.'

'Why was that, do you suppose?' I asked.

'Oh, I'm an old lag, you know. I've done time for assault and battery. I was an obvious choice, since a choice had to be made.'

'Who, in your opinion, were the other candidates for incarceration?' asked Dame Beatrice.

'Well, I don't want to sound unchivalrous, but, speaking quite objectively, I see this as a woman's crime. There were a number of guns in the house –'

I looked up and said, 'I never saw any. Wotton prided himself on not being one of the hunting, shooting and fishing crowd.'

'His father was one of them, though,' said Coberley, 'and he left a little armoury in that room Wotton uses as a den. I don't suppose you have ever seen inside the big cupboard in there. My point is that a man would have shot the girl, not stabbed her in the back.'

I apologised for the interruption, but Dame Beatrice waved a benedictory yellow claw at me and remarked that it was a good thing to get these matters clear. Then she turned again to Coberley and said: 'So you think that a man would have shot Miss Mundy.'

'At least a man would not have needed to stab her in the back, as I said. She was a slight, waif-like little thing whom a man could have strangled with one hand. That would have settled the thing if he thought a shot would be heard.'

'Before we continue this interesting discussion,' said Dame Beatrice, 'apart from your record of violence, what other evidence do you suppose the police have against you? I have my own theories, of course, but what are yours?'

'Oh, that's an easy one,' said this new and, to me, astonishing Coberley. 'It boils down, as I see it, to a question of alibis. Before I was arrested we heard a load of cods-wallop about gangs of town hooligans. They are supposed to have buttered the steps of my house, mugged Gloria Mundy, set fire to the old house and all the rest of it.'

'You mentioned a question of alibis.'

'That's right, so I did. Well, upon thinking things over and also consulting with my lawyer, it seems likely that the men who were at Beeches Lawn can more or less account for one another. I'm the odd man out because, of course, I was over at the school a good deal of the time and, when I hang a notice on the headmaster's door asking not to be disturbed – which, in effect, means I don't want naughty boys brought to me by incompetent masters who can't keep order and on whose behalf I am expected to cane their boys, an operation I dislike intensely and resort to as few times as possible – nobody, not even my wife or my head assistant, can account for my movements. The fact that on such occasions I merely put my feet up, have a quiet drink and a smoke and study the stock market, in which I still have an interest, is neither here nor there. For the space of, say, a couple of hours, I do not exist, so far as is known, and, thus disembodied, could be up to anything, including murder and arson.'

'Excellent,' said Dame Beatrice in an absentminded way which made me think that she had spotted something in all this which might be a help to her. 'To resume our previous topic at the point where I digressed from it, granted that you are right and that the murder of Gloria Mundy was a woman's crime, which woman have you picked for the rôle of villainess?'

'I believe you are laughing at me,' said Coberley, 'but I will answer the question in all seriousness because the fact is that I simply do not know. It could be any single one of them, or even two in collusion.'

'You said that, with the exception of yourself, the men could alibi one another. Could not the women, with the possible exception of your wife, do the same?'

'They could, but I don't think they would. Men will lie themselves black in the face in support of the old school tie. Women have no such mistaken loyalties. A woman will tell little fibs on behalf of a girl friend, such as claiming that the friend was staying the weekend with her when actually the damsel was sharing an illicit bed quite elsewhere, or telling the friend's husband that she was with his wife when she bought a new dress "in the sales for a knockdown price" and then tell the wife to keep her fingers crossed and hope that he won't notice the big hole in their joint account when he goes over the books at the end of the quarter or whenever it is; but, when it comes to the real crunch, women get cold feet and tell the truth willy-nilly.'

'Not all women,' I said.

'There are exceptions to every rule, Stratford.'

'Sorry,' I said. 'Just the chivalrous knight speaking up for a maligned and unjustly treated sex.'

'I gather, Mr Coberley, that you do not share a bank account with your wife,' said Dame Beatrice.

'I might, if most of the money was hers and not mine. As it is, I'm not such a fool. You asked me to pick out the woman who murdered Gloria Mundy. I can't do it. All I know is that, in a serious matter of this kind, women wouldn't connive to give each other alibis.'

'May we have chapter and verse?'

'I imagine, even from the little I saw of her, that Gloria was a red rag to a bull to other women. She had no beauty, either of face or figure, yet, from what I have gathered, men were her cornfield and her vineyard.'

'There was her remarkable hair,' said Dame Beatrice. 'Perhaps that was the attraction. What say you, Mr Stratford?'

'When I buy a horse it will be a strawberry roan,' I said. 'I don't go for piebalds and skewbalds.'

'I gather that both of you were immune to Gloria's charms,' said Dame Beatrice. 'Now, Mr Coberley, line up your suspects.'

'I repeat,' said this new and astonishing man, 'it could have been any one of them. I am perfectly certain that any normal, sex-orientated woman would have declared war on Gloria Mundy at sight. Let us (as you seem to wish this) take the ladies in question one by one, leaving out my wife, who had no fear of female rivalry.'

'I should think not,' I said warmly.

Dame Beatrice cackled and Coberley said in his best headmaster's voice, 'Attend to your work, boy.'

Instead of doing so immediately, I asked a direct and, to my mind, a pertinent question. 'Aren't you taking this being brought to trial seriously?'

'I might, if I were guilty, but I'm not, you see,' he said. 'Sir Ferdinand got me a very light sentence when last I appeared before a jury, and this time I expect to escape without a stain on my character.'

'Sir Ferdinand?' I said blankly.

'My son,' said Dame Beatrice, 'a clever and unscrupulous boy, but it is more fitting that the guilty should escape man's vengeance rather than that the innocent should suffer. I must place it on record, however, that I had no hand in Mr Coberley's choice of a lawyer. Now, client, back to business, if you please. Name your dames and let us have your opinion of each in turn and, if you can manage it, your reason for bringing her under suspicion.'

I could not see how this catalogue was going to help the enquiry, but I trusted that Dame Beatrice had something constructive in mind and

103

that she anticipated that Coberley's opinions would shed some ray of light upon what still seemed to be the impenetrable darkness and mystery which surrounded Gloria Mundy's death.

'Well, my first choice would be Mrs Wotton,' said Coberley. 'It was easy to see that she detested the girl. Wotton and I had a couple of drinks too many when I was at his place one night. This was some time ago, before any of this murder and arson business. I have no doubt I unburdened myself in a way I would not do normally, but so did he, by Jove! I heard the full story of Gloria Mundy's conquest of him and he finished up by begging me to forgive him for bandying a woman's name and saying that he had made a clean breast of the whole affair to his wife before they married.'

'It was Celia Wotton who asked the wretched girl to stay to lunch that day,' I pointed out.

'Yes, because she knew it was the last thing Wotton wanted. It was a mean little way of getting a bit of her own back,' said Coberley.

'Oh, come, now!' I protested. 'Any hostess would have felt bound to do the same.'

'To an uninvited and obviously unwelcome guest? Still, you may be right.'

'After the soup-splashing incident, everybody took it for granted that Miss Mundy had slung her hook. Nobody expected her to be seen at the old house,' I said.

'Nevertheless, that's where she was,' said Dame Beatrice. 'Can you produce any evidence, apart from a somewhat weak motive, for your suspicions of Mrs Wotton?'

'No, I can't. I have no evidence against any of the ladies. The only two I don't suspect at all are my wife and the elderly aunt. I have reasons for excepting these two. Apart from the fact that she later broke her leg, the old lady had scored a signal triumph with her quite disgraceful behaviour at table and was far too pleased with herself to plan any further assault on that young serpent, and my wife, having committed one murder, had the fright of her life when she was brought to trial and is utterly inhibited from murdering anybody else.'

I looked at Dame Beatrice and asked, 'Is that good psychology, Domina?'

'Oh, it could be,' she responded. She turned again to Coberley.

'So you knew your wife killed her first husband?'

'I thought everybody knew it,' he said. 'I was the chief witness for the prosecution, you know. The deed was done in my office. Marigold was my secretary. Her husband had come to kick up a fuss about what he had made up his mind was our relationship with one another. I need hardly tell you that there was nothing in the least improper about it. I treated her like a daughter, but that is all. I am twenty-five years older than she is and, beyond admiring her beauty and finding her knowledge of Spanish, her native language, very useful in my business – for I had large interests in South America, particularly with the Argentine – I was (and still am, if it comes to that) merely a father figure in her life.'

'So her hot Spanish blood got the better of her when her husband came to your office,' I said.

'I suppose so. I heard the shot and burst in to find her with the gun in her hand and the fellow lying on the carpet. Of course I wasn't going to admit to anybody what I had seen. I said, "You silly girl! Now look at what you've done! Drop the gun beside him." '

'Did she always carry a gun?' I asked. He took no notice.

'Of course there were voices outside and soon a knock on the door,' he said. 'I did not invite anybody in, but, of course, it opened and a scared typist asked whether everything was all right. I replied that a man had just shot himself and that she was to telephone for the police. That's the whole story. When Marigold was acquitted I married her and bought the school after I had changed my name.'

'You were not alarmed at becoming the husband of such a volatile young creature?' asked Dame Beatrice.

'Oh, no. Things came out, you know. He was an absolute waster, an undischarged bankrupt and a chap who had bought the gun and threatened suicide with it more than once. There were witnesses who supported Marigold's statement about that. Of course there were her prints on the gun superimposed on his, so the defence relied mainly on a story of a struggle for the gun which then went off and killed the fellow. Of course I was called for the prosecution, but they didn't get much joy out of me. You can't run a business as successful as mine was without being able to tell a good big thumping lie or two when the need arises, but I really think it was Marigold's outstanding beauty and a sort of defencelessness about her which really swayed the jury; neither could the prosecution find anybody who could produce evidence of previous quarrels between the husband and wife, although I'm pretty sure they led a cat and dog life. In fact, they both lived on Marigold's salary, which I bumped up from time to time because, in a fatherly or avuncular way, I was very fond of her. I used to take her out to meals quite a lot. I got the impression that she often went hungry.'

'Which of them had brought the gun to your office?' I could not help asking.

This time he answered me. 'She said that she had. Her story was that he had been in a deeply depressed mood when she left for work that morning and she had not dared to leave him in the house with it.'

'And which of them do *you* think had toted it along?'

'Oh, *he* had, of course. He had come to the office to shoot *me*. She had asked him for a divorce, you see. She told me exactly what had happened as soon as we were married. She saw him produce the gun and simply held out her hand for it, took it and shot him.'

'Just like that?' I said.

'Just like that.'

'But why?'

'Because he had threatened that one day he would turn up at the office and shoot me. When she was acquitted I took her straight off to the south of France for a year and we were married as soon as we came back to England.'

At a signal from Dame Beatrice I had written down none of this story. I was astonished, in fact, that he had told it. I resumed my task, however, when Dame Beatrice said, 'Well, we have mentioned some of the women who were at Beeches Lawn. What about the others?'

'I don't see any way of choosing between them,' said Coberley. 'The two unmarried girls are less likely murderers than Mrs Wotton, perhaps, simply because they were not only younger than she, but, because of that very fact, possibly had their fiancés under firm control. A fiancée is always stronger in most respects than a wife. No, on the whole I plump for Celia Wotton.'

'What Coberley does not know,' I said to Dame Beatrice when we got outside, 'is that Kate McMaster had exactly the same motive as Celia Wotton for detesting Gloria Mundy. Before his marriage McMaster had a caper with her. One of the husbands-to-be picked her up at a night-club, the other on board a cruise liner, but that seems to have been the only difference. Kate McMaster would have known the address of Beeches Lawn because McMaster came to see me there.'

'Yes, but she could not have known that Miss Mundy was to go there.'

'Did you get anything helpful from Coberley?' I asked.

'I found the whole interview very interesting,' she replied, 'particularly the importance he attaches to the eleventh Commandment.'

'Oh, about telling lies? In time of trouble thou shalt tell a lie, a good lie, and stick to it. Yes, indeed. Incidentally, I had to exercise a lot of self-control to avoid telling him what I thought of him for accusing Celia Wotton. I respect and admire her and it was hurtful to think that anybody should accuse her of stabbing another woman in the back.'

'Some women do it metaphorically, of course. He was very frank in confessing that he could not furnish himself with any kind of an alibi, but, as I think we are agreed, no alibi is of use, either to the police or the person under suspicion, until we know when the murder actually took place. Being a shrewd man, he has worked that out for himself. Have you your luggage with you?'

'Yes. I'm not going back to my hotel – or, rather, to one of McMaster's hotels. I have finished the job I was doing for him and shall send him the last bit of my work tomorrow when I've gone through it and done any necessary typing at home. I will also type out today's shorthand and send it to you.'

'If you can spare the time, why not bring it to me and stay for a couple of days? We can find plenty of material for conversation and Laura will like to hear our combined account of today's visit. I am interested in Mr Coberley's assertion that the murder was committed by a woman.'

'What is your own opinion about that? You said that women were capable metaphorically of stabbing one another in the back, but it might be much more difficult for them to bring themselves to do it physically, don't you think?'

'It might depend upon the sharpness of the weapon, the physical energy of the murderess and her knowledge of anatomy,' said Dame Beatrice, pretending to misunderstand me.

'I recoil from the idea of a woman plunging cold steel into another woman,' I said.

'A typical masculine reaction, but the squeamishness becomes you. Shall I look forward to seeing you tomorrow, then, at lunch? Can you get your work finished by then?'

'Oh, yes, easily, and I can post it to McMaster on my way to you.'

'Before we meet again, I should be glad if you would turn over in your mind everything which happened between Gloria Mundy's invasion – I use the word advisedly, for that is what it seems to have been – and the discovery of the charred body. Will you do that and prepare yourself to answer any questions which it may occur to me to put to you?'

'Certainly, and thank you for the invitation. Has Coberley convinced you of his own innocence?'

'By no means. The evidence against him may be slight, but it must be taken into account.'

12
Recapitulation with Surprise Ending

I enjoyed my two days at the Stone House. The three of us discussed the salient facts of what had taken place at Beeches Lawn so far as our knowledge of them went, and I charged my memory with making out a timetable in the hope that it would reveal to us the day on which the murder had taken place.

'But it won't tell us *where* it took place,' I said. 'It could have happened in the old house or somewhere quite other and the body brought back to be burnt. That has been obvious from the beginning. If only they knew where the stabbing happened, the police might not have seen fit to arrest Coberley.'

'Let us have your timetable,' said Dame Beatrice. 'You were at Beeches Lawn before the rest of us arrived and you stayed longer than anybody else.'

'Well,' I said, 'I got down to Beeches Lawn on the Thursday. I had taken some work with me and I was all set for a quiet, pleasant week. Anthony seemed glad to see me and Celia was charming, so that was fine.

'Friday was an equally peaceful day. Anthony showed me round the estate, but then (to my regret at the time) I heard that an influx of weekend visitors was expected and on the Saturday they began to arrive.

'On Sunday I was shown the interior of the old house. Coberley, who had the key, took me inside, warned me about the rickety staircase and showed me the nude portrait. I thought at once – at least, I believe I did – of Gloria Mundy, whose remarkable hair McMaster, the man I was working for, had described to me shortly before.

Anyway, the picture was not a portrait of Gloria, but it must have been that of an ancestress of hers, and I'm sure it lends credence to her claim to be a distant relative of Anthony Wotton. It seems to me that his great-grandfather had an illegitimate child by the girl in the portrait and that the peculiar hair had been passed down to Gloria.'

'Miss Brockworth, you told me, thought that Miss Mundy wore a wig in imitation of the hair in the portrait,' said Dame Beatrice.

'Then the wig was a fairly recent acquisition,' I said. 'She certainly didn't wear a wig when her lover or lovers used to wash her hair for her.'

'As the hair seems to have been the only means of establishing the identity of the corpse, I must still regard it with some suspicion,' said Dame Beatrice.

'But, if the body wasn't Gloria's, whose could it have been?'

'I am not saying that it was not Gloria's. All the same, I think the police would be well advised to check their lists of missing persons. If it should transpire that the body is not that of Gloria Mundy, some part of the case against Mr Coberley must collapse.'

'It's weak enough already, in my opinion,' I said. 'Shall I go on? On the Sunday two other things happened, neither of which seems particularly significant. You, Dame Beatrice, had a session with Aunt Eglantine in private and then were called away, and McMaster telephoned to ask me to meet him as there were one or two points to discuss concerning the hotel brochures I was working on. Anthony and Celia preferred that he be asked to come to Beeches Lawn, as he, Anthony and I had been in college together. He was invited to bring his wife with him, but he came without her.

'Meanwhile a more important thing happened on the Sunday. Gloria Mundy turned up, was invited to stay to lunch and did not get further than the apportioning of the plates of soup because the outrageous behaviour of Miss Eglantine drove her from the table.'

'I am sorry I missed such a dramatic episode, but I was called away even sooner than I expected,' said Dame Beatrice.

'McMaster also missed it, since he did not appear until lunch was over and Gloria Mundy (so far as anybody knew) was well and truly off the premises. Well, two of the younger guests, Roland Thornbury and Kay Shortwood, had planned to go home that evening and McMaster was not intending to stay the night, but the storm settled all that. Roland and Kay had to abandon their car and come back and the Wottons persuaded McMaster not to attempt a journey because of flooded roads.

'When they got back to Beeches Lawn, Roland and Kay told this strange story of having seen Gloria at one of the windows of the old house, and the story was borne out by Miss Eglantine next day when she went there in the morning to look at the picture and ran into Gloria, who told her the picture was upstairs. Most rashly, with her weight, she tried the stairs, brought part of them down and broke her leg.'

'So that brings us to Monday morning,' said Laura.

'Oh, wait a moment. No, I think it brings us to Tuesday. Roland spent Monday morning in bed and, if I remember correctly, the picture was mentioned on Monday, but the old lady did not go to the old house until Tuesday after breakfast. I think it must have been on the Monday that Celia had her first row with Anthony. They had more than one before they decided to call it a day.'

'About Gloria?' asked Laura. 'The rows, I mean.'

'Yes, about Gloria. Anthony, the ass, had told Celia all about his little affair and Celia, I suppose, had stored up her ammunition, and it only needed Gloria to turn up the way she did for the spark to ignite the gunpowder.'

'And after Tuesday you would have been the only guest left in the house, I suppose,' said Dame Beatrice.

'I was due to stay until Thursday in any case. After the bonfire and then the discovery of the body, Anthony and Celia welcomed the idea of having somebody else in the place, I think. I've left out the accident to Marigold Coberley, but it has to be mentioned because the police believe it was Coberley's motive for the murder.'

'I don't think we've cleared the air,' said Laura. 'If the murder was committed *before* Mrs Coberley had her fall, bang goes that motive, as I think we've all agreed.'

At this point I had to confront the dilemma in which I found myself. I gave it due consideration, conscious that Dame Beatrice's sharp black eyes were on me. She came to my assistance.

'There is something troubling you,' she said. 'A matter of conscience?'

I decided to trust her.

'Well,' I said, 'it seems to me that, if it comes to a question of motive, Anthony Wotton had at least as strong a one as Coberley. Some people might think it stronger.'

'I wonder why Miss Brockworth told you the story about the baby?' said Laura. 'Was it just a shot at Wotton, do you think? I'll tell you one thing,' she went on, before I could answer. 'She sounds to me about as dotty as they come. Suppose *she* was the one who stabbed Gloria and then broke her leg *after* the deed was done? Isn't that a possibility?'

'I don't think so,' I said. 'She could have committed the murder, as you say, but she couldn't have started the fire. She was most certainly in hospital when that happened.'

'Can you remember the details of the soup incident?' asked Dame Beatrice. 'I can envisage the scene when the bread was thrown, but what happened immediately after that? Did Miss Mundy leap from her chair and rush precipitately from the room?'

'It amounted to that. She was sitting between William Underedge and Roland Thornbury. They both jumped out of the way and then Underedge began to mop down Gloria's sweater with his table napkin, but she pushed him away, and Celia got up and went to her and said, "Oh, dear! Come along to the bathroom and sponge down." Gloria wouldn't have any of that, either, but flung her own table napkin on to the table where most of the soup had gone, rushed out and we heard the bang as the front door slammed. Then there was a general upset while Underedge and Thornbury attended to the one or two splashes they had received and the tablecloth was changed and fresh table napkins supplied to the two young men and after that the rest of the lunch was served.'

'The windows of the dining-room, I recall,' said Dame Beatrice, 'look out upon the lawn and a broad path divides the lawn from the frontage of the house. Did anybody notice whether Miss Mundy went past the window?'

'I have never heard that anybody did. I think we were all too flum-moxed by what had happened to give an eye to anything but the mess and the mopping-up operations. I shouldn't think she went past the windows, though, as she landed up in the old house. I saw her arrive and she came from the direction of the schoolboys' playing-field, but the old house lies in the opposite direction,' I said.

'I wonder why she chose that way in? One would suppose that the road from the town was shorter by way of the old house rather than by the way of the playing-field.'

'I imagine she came from the railway station, asked for directions to Beeches Lawn and was shown the lane which passes what used to be the convent. I don't think she had ever been to Beeches Lawn before, you see.'

'I noticed gardeners at work when I arrived,' said Dame Beatrice. 'No doubt the police have questioned them.'

'They have questioned all the servants, I believe, but I expect the gardener and his boy were having their midday meal at the same time as we were having lunch. I doubt whether they would have seen any-thing of Gloria.'

'If she had not been to Beeches Lawn before, how did she know about the picture?'

'My impression is that, at some time while he was having his affair with her, Wotton had told Gloria about the picture and its resem-blance to herself, and she went to the old house either to look at it or to steal it. It may well have been the latter since, according to Miss Eglantine, there was no picture to be seen when she herself went over there to take a look at it. My view is that Gloria had already stolen it. I don't see any reason why she should have taken it upstairs, as she told Aunt Eglantine she had done. I doubt whether she would have risked climbing that staircase, lightweight though she was. She probably hoped, after the soup incident, that Aunt Eg would break her neck on it instead of her leg.'

'Reverting to the blackmailing photograph, did you obtain any description of the party who had brought the baby along?'

'Wotton referred to her as a waif, I think, that's all.'

'Could the description, so far as it goes, fit Miss Mundy herself?'

'Well, she was a meagre, skinny little thing, so perhaps it could. I see what you mean. You think the other girl is a myth and that it really *was* Gloria's baby. But, if it was, and there was no accomplice present, who took the photograph?'

'Some obliging and innocent passer-by was pressed into service, perhaps. People are wonderfully kind.'

'Well, I believe Anthony's story,' I said stoutly.

'Dame Beatrice thinks,' said Laura Gavin, 'that Mr Wotton is any-thing but in the clear and *I* think the police might do worse than take a look at Celia, who obviously hated Gloria's guts. One also has to allow for person or persons unknown. Suppose the police are right and there *were* squatters in the old house? Might they not have objected in a forceful manner to Gloria's invasion of the premises? They could have been responsible for the bonfire, you know. It wasn't their own property they were burning down.'

'You knew of the existence of Miss Mundy before you went to Beeches Lawn, did you not?' said Dame Beatrice to me.

'Yes, as I've told you, from old Hara-kiri. As soon as she pulled off the cap she was wearing when I first caught sight of her from my bed-room window, I concluded who she must be. That hair was unmistakable.'

'Brings us back to the wig,' said Laura, 'and all the weary work to do again.'

'Between the time when Anthony and McMaster first fell into her toils and the time of her visit to Beeches Lawn,' I said, 'she might have taken to wearing a wig. I mean, some people go grey very early in life and some illnesses lead to premature baldness, don't they? Wouldn't either of those explanations account for the wig?'

I was surprised, when I got back to my flat, to find Hara-kiri waiting for me in the caretaker's little den. I took him up to my rooms and poured drinks.

'Something wrong with the brochures?' I asked, handing him his glass.

'Lord, no! We're very pleased with them and we particularly like the photographs and the very clear road-maps. You've done an excellent job for us.' He took a deep draught of whisky, stared into his glass, tossed off the rest of the drink and then said, 'Corin, old lad, would you regard me as a man who was likely to see ghosts?'

I gave him the time-honoured one about that depending upon what other spirits he had been acquainting himself with at the time. Then I recharged his glass. He set it down and said, 'I'm perfectly serious. I've seen the ghost of Gloria Mundy.'

'You can't have done.'

'She's dead, isn't she?'

'One assumes so.'

'I mean, there's been an inquest and the body has been identified as hers.'

'Wotton and I identified it; not an experience I would want too often.'

'And the medical evidence was given that she had been stabbed?'

'You seem to have read your newspapers.'

'And that the murderer had attempted to cover up the crime by burning the body?'

'Quite correct, old man.'

'Well, then, I've seen her ghost.'

'Where?'

'In Trends, that dress shop. I was in there the other day.'

'Oh, come, come, come!' I said. 'What would Gloria's ghost be doing in Trends?'

'Selling evening gowns. She used to work there, you know.'

I looked at him with the deepest concern and asked him whether he had ever had a really bad knock on the head.

'I expect I got a kick or two on it. You do sometimes when you go down in front of a forward rush, but that was donkey's years ago. It's never affected me except in the most temporary way. This wasn't hallucination, Corin,' he said earnestly.

'Ghosts *are* hallucination. Tell me more,' I said. 'Were you under the influence at the time?'

13
The Revenant

He shook his head and said, 'There isn't any more to tell.'

'Of course there is. Chapter and verse, man, chapter and verse!'

'I'm no good at that sort of thing. It's your department to fill in the padding, not mine.'

'All right, I'll help you out. What were you doing in Trends? I thought they catered exclusively – and I can say *that* again when I think of their prices – exclusively for the sex which we prize above rubies.'

'That's right. Kate had dragged me there so that I could buy her a couple of evening dresses.'

'Ah, now we're off. Begin at the beginning. This sounds like good stuff and I may be able to get some copy out of it.'

'No naming any names, then. Yes, well, Kate and I go out quite a bit and she came to the conclusion, as women are all too apt to do, that she had nothing fit to wear. I suggested that I should supply her with funds and that she should take a woman friend with her and chase round the shops, but, as usual, she insisted on taking me along and we went to Trends. There I saw Gloria's ghost.'

'Trends wouldn't allow ghosts in their exclusive emporium. I suppose you thought you recognised the hair.'

'As a matter of fact, no. This girl was entirely black-haired and was wearing a black frock and she had a dead-white face.'

'Well, there you are, then. She was a real girl, not a ghost and certainly not Gloria.'

McMaster took up his drink, looked at it and put it down again. 'It was Gloria and she was a ghost. Look, Corin, in the old days I wined and dined Gloria, I took her to ballet and the theatre, I went to Paris with her – God knows what it did to my money, but I told you about that, I expect – and I slept with her. I couldn't possibly be mistaken. Besides, although people can change their hair and their complexion and a man can grow a beard or shave one off, there is one thing neither man nor woman can alter, and that is the colour of their eyes and the way those eyes are set in the head. I know you can do a lot with eye-shadow and theatrical make-up, but you can't really disguise the basics. Gloria had cats' eyes, green as green glass and utterly without humour, kindness or pity. This ghost had those eyes.'

'A chance likeness, that's all. But even if you're right' – I remembered the story of the dead girl's hair which got scorched but not burnt, whereas her face was so scorched and blackened as to be not only a thing of horror but unrecognisable as a human countenance, and I began to feel a thrill of excitement – 'even if you're right,' I repeated, 'it was no ghost that you saw. It must have been Gloria in the flesh.'

'No,' he said obstinately, 'it was her ghost. I can prove it. It disappeared.'

'Disappeared? You mean it recognised you and melted into thin air?'

'It amounted to that. We went to the part of the shop which Kate wanted to look in and this black-haired, black-clad, white-faced thing appeared from nowhere – '

'No, from a fitting-room or from behind a rack of clothes. I know these dress shops.'

McMaster ignored this.

'I couldn't believe my eyes. I really thought at first it was Gloria in the flesh,' he said. 'Well, I didn't want any Auld Lang Syne stuff with Kate there, so I turned my back and began to look at some dresses, and I heard Gloria's ghost say the usual 'Can I help you, madam?' or something of that sort, and I knew it was a disembodied voice, not a human one.'

'But, my dear chap, they tell me ghosts can't speak unless you address them first, and even then they don't always bother to answer.

Seriously, though, this girl didn't look like Gloria and didn't sound like Gloria, so what?'

'All right, have it your way. All I know is that, when I half turned to have another peep, a tall, buxom blonde was with Kate and there was no sign of Gloria at all. What do you make of that?'

'Easy,' I said. 'These days you give an impression of opulence beyond that of the Great Cham himself. The blonde was the senior assistant in that department and wasn't going to let a lucrative sale, with its nice fat commission, get away from her. Kissing goes by seniority in these establishments and the top girls pull their rank, same like everywhere else. The blonde must have gone through the secret motions which meant "Hop it; this is my pigeon for the plucking", and the girl you mistook for Gloria sank without trace. Probably just slipped behind a rack of long dresses.'

'It *sounds* all right when you put it like that, but it *isn't* all right. If it wasn't Gloria's ghost, it was Gloria herself, as I thought at first, and that, as we know, is unthinkable.'

I told him that I was beginning to consider it not so unthinkable after all. What had Wotton and I had to go on, when, separately, we had identified that very dead creature? Nothing but hair of two colours and the declaration from two unrelated and, one would suppose, disinterested sources that Gloria had been seen inside the old house after she was supposed to have left Beeches Lawn many hours previously. I reminded him that, upon his arrival there, Gloria had not been in the house, certainly, but that he himself had seen her in the grounds.

'Quite likely she had been hanging around hoping that one of you would come out and offer her a lift to the station, so there was nothing much in that,' he said. 'It only proves that she was still alive *at that time.*'

'Well, if you saw her in Trends, she was still alive then, too,' I said, 'but don't you think it was some other girl who had eyes and a figure similar to those of Gloria? You had read of Gloria's death, you had reminded yourself of your previous association with her and, in other words, she was very much in the forefront of your mind. Add to that the fact that you had Kate with you and you were going to buy clothes for her. Did you ever buy clothes for Gloria?'

'Yes, of course, and was nearly beggared by Trends' prices, although, as an employee, she got a discount and I was never present.' He looked hopefully at me. 'So it wasn't a ghost. All the same – '

'All the same, it wasn't Gloria either. Besides, from what little I saw of her at Beeches Lawn, her two-coloured hair was her only claim to distinction and I don't believe she would have sacrificed it. Snap out of it, old man.'

'You make out a good case,' he said, 'but – well, I dunno.'

We had another drink before he left. I could tell that I had not convinced him, but I remembered him from the old days as an obstinate fellow who, once he got an idea into his head, retained it against all opposition or argument. All the same, his 'I wined and dined Gloria, I took her to ballet and the theatre, I went to Paris with her . . . I slept with her' showed me that his association with her had lasted longer and had been much closer than I had suspected.

I was sufficiently intrigued to carry the matter further. I was at a loose end for a little while. The brochures were finished, I had been extremely well-paid and I was not quite ready to get back to my writing, so, having both time and money on my hands, I thought it might be a graceful act to buy Celia and Anthony a little present and send it with a note of my gratitude for their hospitality. It would also give me a chance to check McMaster's story.

On the ground floor at Trends I found a very nice set of apostle spoons and decided that this would be appropriate. The packaging of them was elegant and distinctive, so, armed with the box, I took the lift to the floor where the female fashions were displayed, dangled the package as a guarantee of my *bona fides* and was taken in charge by a young creature with almost silver hair. The package, however, had been spotted by McMaster's magnificent blonde, who came swanning up and immediately superseded the youngster.

'I wonder,' I said, 'whether I could have the young lady who served me the last time I was in here? She proved very helpful.'

'Oh, yes?'

120

'She was a thin girl with black hair and a very white make-up. Green-eyed, I think, and full of helpful suggestions.'

'Oh, yes?'

'Could I have her again? I'm pretty hopeless at choosing things for my wife and this is to be a surprise.'

'Oh, yes? Well, I am afraid the assistant you require is no longer with us.'

'Oh, dear! I was relying on her as to size.'

'Size?'

'Well, you see, yes. She was just about the same height and size as my wife, so I thought I would get her to try on a few things, as it were, to give me some idea.'

'I am sorry. That assistant left us the day before yesterday. Perhaps – ' She made an imperious gesture and the silver-haired siren came up again. I smiled and shook my head.

'Nothing for it but to bring my wife along,' I said. 'Rather does in the surprise aspect, but there it is.'

'I am sorry we cannot help you.'

'There is always a next time. Thanks very much. Hope I haven't been a bother.'

'Not at all. *Good* morning.' She spotted a customer and glided away. I found myself left with Silverhair.

'I'm looking for a girl named Gloria,' I said. 'I'm really a plain-clothes police officer and – '

'So that's why she skipped! All I know is that she lived somewhere Culvert Green way. In a hostel of some sort, I think, but I never went there. Police! Coo! I should never have thought it. She seemed such a nice sort of girl. Domremy was her surname, very posh, and she was always ladylike, and never any nasty snide remarks about the other girls. We thought she left because she had an argument with Lady Muck. Police! Well, really!'

I took it that she referred to the magnificent blonde under the title of Lady Muck.

'So Gloria had a dust-up with the supervisor or whatever she's called,' I said. 'You are sure her name was Gloria?'

'Of course I am. Sorry, a customer. Excuse me, please.'

The lead she had given me seemed too promising to ignore. I decided that I would try my luck at Culvert Green. It seemed certain now that Anthony and I had wrongly identified the corpse. My first thought was to telephone Dame Beatrice, but, although I hesitated outside the first public callbox I came to after I had left the shop, I changed my mind. It would be something really to report if I could say that I had actually tracked down Gloria and that she was alive after all.

It then occurred to me that the proper procedure would be to telephone the police, but I soon dismissed that idea, too. All that I could tell them was that an assistant saleswoman at Trends in London had been recognised as Gloria Mundy, that she had left in a hurry and that, although she had disguised herself to some extent, she had kept the name Gloria, had been of the required build and had been seen some weeks after her supposed death.

If I told the police all this, though, they would need to contact McMaster and, if he decided, after all, to stick to his ghost story, the police undoubtedly would ignore both of us – if, indeed, they did not doubt our sanity or decide that we were trying to perpetrate a hoax at their expense.

I had lunch at a restaurant and took a bus to Culvert Green. It is a pleasant suburb out on the Kent border not all that far from Blackheath. There were streets of small shops, but along the main road the houses had been built as large, middle-class, Victorian family dwellings with front gardens which were far enough from gate to doorway to give some privacy from the curiosity of passers-by.

Most of the houses had basements with their own steep, narrow steps leading to the servants' entrances and flights of broad stone steps leading up to the front doors. Above the basements the houses rose in three storeys; they had large bay windows on the first floor, large Georgian-type windows on the floor above this, and much smaller, rather mean-looking windows on the top floor.

Some of the houses had been turned into flats, others had become business premises and their owners had taken down the street wall and gates (from which, in any case, the iron railings had been removed

122

during the war) and had concreted what had been the front lawns and turned them into parking-spaces for the workers' and management's cars.

The other three houses past which I walked were a YWCA hostel, a hall of residence for college students and a more imposing mansion than either. This was a guest house called the Clovelly Private Hotel.

From what I had heard of Gloria I thought that this was more likely to be her choice than a YWCA hostel, so I mounted the steps and went in through an open front door which led into a small vestibule. Beyond this were swing doors. I pushed in and on my left there was the reception desk and behind it at a small table a woman and a girl of about nineteen were having a cup of tea.

They did not appear to have noticed my entrance, in spite of the fact that one of the swing doors had given a slight moan, so I coughed to attract attention. The older woman looked up.

'Sorry,' she said, 'no vacancies. Residents only, and we're full.'

'I don't need accommodation. I am looking for my sister and the place where she worked gave me this address. I am from the Argentine.' (I suppose my subconscious mind brought this country uppermost, since I had been told that Coberley had had business interests there.) 'So we have not met for years and she may be married by now. The name is M—' I was about to say Mundy, but caught the word back and substituted 'Malvern'.

'No guest of that name here.'

'She wrote to me that she was engaged to a man named Domremy. Would a Mrs Domremy mean anything to you? As I remember my sister, she was very slightly built and had red hair and a pale complexion. Sometimes she dyed part of her hair black, sometimes all of it was black.'

The woman shook her head, but the girl, who was still seated in the background, said, 'It couldn't be, could it?'

'Couldn't be what?' asked the woman.

'*You* know. That case in the papers. It said *she* had red hair one side of her head and black the other.'

'Of course it couldn't be her. We don't get ourselves mixed up with murder and that kind of thing.' She turned to me again. 'We don't know anything about a Miss Malvern or a Mrs Whatever name you said.' She turned her back on me and went back to her cup of tea.

'One moment,' I said peremptorily.

'Well?'

'I am a police officer. If you know anything whatever about the woman with the red and black hair and do not disclose it, you will be hindering me in the execution of my duty, and that is an indictable offence.'

If either of them had asked me for my credentials at this point, I should have been stymied, but fortunately neither of them thought of it, any more than the girl in Trends had done. The older woman came back to the counter.

'She *was* here, perhaps, if we're talking about the same person,' she said, 'but please don't ever mention it, us not wanting the reporters and the notoriety, and her hair was always dark while she was here. She called herself Parkstone and we never saw her with anything but dark-brown hair, not really black.'

'Parkstone?' What imp of mischief had been at work here, I wondered. 'When did she leave?'

'Oh, that would have been a fortnight ago.'

'Do you know where she worked?'

'Oh, yes, she worked at Trends in the West End.'

'Did she ever have visitors?'

'Not that I know of. I shouldn't think her sort would have wanted them if the police wanted *her*. No wonder she left here, if you were on her track.'

'Did she leave anything behind?'

'Oh, no. We're fully furnished, so she only took her clothes with her. There was nothing else. Look, we can't help you, so you'll keep us out of the papers, won't you? This place is my livelihood, you see, mine and my daughter's.' She indicated the girl at the table.

'We are very discreet,' I said. 'I shan't need to trouble you again, I'm sure. Did this Miss Parkstone leave a forwarding address for letters?'

'Oh, no, nothing of that sort. She would have left it with the post-office, I expect.'

I had no idea what to do next. I seemed to have come to a dead end almost as soon as I had started. I walked somewhat disconsolately to the bus stop, but while I stood there I thought of one more thing which I could do, although, in my chastened state of mind, I did not think anything would come of it. I left the bus stop and walked down a side street to the post-office, not really believing for a moment that Gloria would have left an address there if she was on the run, as now seemed more than likely.

It was one of those places which combines postal business with keeping a little shop. This one sold stationery, birthday cards, sello-tape, string, paperbacks, pencils and pencil-sharpeners, paperclips, india-rubbers and other oddments, so I made a few purchases and then went to the post-office counter and bought some stamps.

'I want to send birthday cards to my nieces,' I said, 'but they seem to have moved from their hotel. Would you have a forwarding address for Parkstone, Mundy and Domremy?'

The name Mundy appeared to mean nothing to the elderly woman behind the wire mesh. Perhaps she did not read the papers.

'We have one for Parkstone,' she said. 'Where did your niece live? We don't usually give people's addresses to strangers.'

'Until fairly recently she was staying at the Clovelly Private Hotel near here.'

'Oh, that's all right, then. You can't be a stranger. I'll write it down for you.'

I began to see how con-men make a living. I took the bit of paper she handed me, thanked her, bought a ball of string and some fancy wrap-ping paper from the girl who had already served me, added these to my other small purchases and then bought a carrier bag. My camouflage, I decided, had been foolproof. I tucked away the precious piece of paper and went back to the bus stop.

That evening I wrote to Dame Beatrice to tell her what McMaster had told me and to give her an account of my experiences in Culvert Green. I posted it so that it would go off by the first collection next morning. Then I looked at the piece of paper the woman at the post-office had given me. It bore the address of a house in the little town of Chaynorth in Sussex.

I knew Chaynorth pretty well. One of McMaster's hotels was just outside it, so I had explored it and all the countryside round it when I was working on the brochures. I promised myself a pleasant day out when I went to make enquiries about the nomadic Parkstone, Domremy and Gloria Mundy.

14
Unexpected Developments

This time, of course, I took the car. It was an easy and pleasant run from London. I decided to have lunch in the town and then find the house I wanted.

There were two hotels, the White Hart, built on the foundations of an abbey guest-house, and a quiet Georgian building – quiet, that is to say, because it was in a side street and not on the main road through the town – called Bartlemy's. I suppose I could have gone a little way out and got myself a free, and possibly a better, lunch at McMaster's hotel, but this seemed rather like scrounging, so I resisted what, I will admit, was a temptation and settled for the White Hart.

The hotel was in the high street opposite the old court house where, as I had stated in the brochure, the assizes used to be held, so at one time the White Hart had been much patronised by lawyers. Inside the place one stepped straight into a story by Charles Dickens. There was a heavy, homely, slightly musty atmosphere, the bar was in the charge of a dragon who could have been Mrs Squeers in person, and the dining-room, into which I peeped before ordering a drink, was dim, dark-wainscoted and furnished with large mahogany tables and with chairs of the kind our great-grandfathers probably had in the dining-rooms of their gloomy Victorian homes. On the walls were heavily framed portraits of whiskered gentlemen in Dickensian collars and cravats, and over the mantelpiece, below which a coal fire was burning, hung a vast picture portraying a heavy-featured gentleman in the wig and robes of a judge.

I ordered a drink from the dragon. I would have liked a cocktail, but I met an eye which apparently dared me to ask for such a thing, so I ordered a dry sherry. It turned out to be about double the size served in other bars and no dearer.

'You'll be staying for lunch, I suppose,' she said. Nervously I replied that I would like to have lunch. 'Then make that drink last,' she said. 'One o'clock's the time we serve. You'd better see the head waiter. He'll book you if there's room. It's market day. He'll be in the garden. Put your drink down. I'll keep an eye on it.'

'Which way is the garden?'

'Through there.' She pointed to an archway on my left. I abandoned the sherry to her guardianship, went through the archway and traversed a vast, panelled room hung with pictures of hunting scenes and decorated with post-horns, whips, deers' heads, stuffed pheasants and a giant pike, the last two items in glass cases.

Passing through this mausoleum, I found another door, which opened on to a wooden balcony. From the balcony a long flight of wooden steps with a handrail led down into a long, narrow garden. This was given over mostly to fruit trees now denuded of their produce, but in a border on the right-hand side of a narrow path were some tatty, dreary-looking, bronze and yellow chrysanthemums, about the most uninspiring inflorescences I have ever seen, I think.

Near the end of the garden two elderly men were standing. The taller, whom I took to be one of the hotel guests, was wearing a smoking-jacket and black and grey plaid trousers; the other had on a winged collar and a black frock coat. The old gentleman in the smoking-jacket addressed me.

'Too late for the plums, I'm afraid,' he said.

'I didn't come for plums,' I said. 'I wanted to book a table for lunch.'

'Ah,' said the other old man, 'certainly, sir. Come along while I look at my list. I can't promise you a table to yourself. Our tables are for six or eight persons, and our lunches are popular, sir, very popular.'

'That's all right. I'm a writer. I like company,' I told him. 'One listens and learns.'

'We used to get the lawyers,' he said, preceding me along the narrow path, 'but not now. They've moved the assizes to Bigsey. A pity, sir. Oh, dear! The stories those lawyers could tell! Quite hair-raising, some of them. Other times it was as much as I could do to keep a straight face as a young waiter. Very hilarious, sir, lawyers, and very improper at times. Worse than doctors, I'd say. Will you mount the steps first, sir? I shall be slower than you. The gentleman you saw me with is the owner of this hotel. He misses the lawyers sadly.'

As we walked through the long lounge with its trophies, he went on, 'A writer, did you say, sir? We have a lady of your calling lunching here for the next fortnight. Dinner, too, so I have managed to squeeze in a little table for her, as our regulars are mostly gentlemen, but there would be room for two if she gave permission.'

He accepted a large book from the formidable barmaid, scanned the day's entries and asked me my name. He inscribed it and said, 'One o'clock, sir, please, and your place reserved only until one-fifteen. We are popular, you see.' I picked up my sherry, which the barmaid had covered with a clean beermat and turned to see a young woman standing behind me. 'This is the lady writer. Mr Stratford, miss. Miss Parkstone, sir,' said the waiter.

'Good Lord!' I said. 'Imogen!'

'Good gracious me!' said the girl. 'William, put Mr Stratford at my table if he is staying for lunch.'

'What will you drink?' I asked.

'My usual, please, Mabel.'

'If you like to upset your liver, it's no business of mine,' said the barmaid. 'This gentleman had more sense.' She juggled with bottles and a shaker. We took our drinks into the lounge and seated ourselves in armchairs beneath a particularly fine set of antlers.

'So it was you,' I said. 'How came you to be serving in a dress shop – viz., to wit, Trends?'

'To get material for a book, of course. I got the idea from P.G. Wodehouse. Do you remember Rosie M. Banks?'

'Oh, the female novelist who worked as a waitress in a gentlemen's club to get material for *Mervyn Keene, Clubman?*'

'Exactly. Well, it struck me as such a good idea that I thought I would try it.'

'Monica Dickens tried it, and with signal success. This place rather brings Dickens to mind, don't you think? Of course, Monica's accounts of her experiences were autobiographical.'

'Don't deviate. What's all this about Trends? What were you doing among the ladies' dresses? I didn't know you were married.'

'I'm not.'

'Oho!'

'And not "Oho" either. I am now an amateur detective. I was merely sleuthing at Trends. I was looking for traces of Gloria Mundy.'

'That woman whose body was found in the ashes of a bonfire? How on earth did you get mixed up in that awful business?'

'Never mind that for the moment. It's a long story and it will keep. Let's talk about you. I nearly dropped dead when the woman at the post-office at Culvert Green had a forwarding address for Parkstone. I thought coincidence was playing even more of a joke than usual.'

'I called myself Domremy at Trends, but I thought I had better come clean in the hotel register and at the post-office.'

'Just as well to avoid unnecessary complications.' I looked at her as the autumn sun brightened that otherwise depressing room and made gold lights in her fine-spun, dark-brown hair.

'Why aren't you pale and interesting?' I demanded. 'I was told that you had a whiter-than-white face, black hair, and cats' eyes like green glass when you were at Trends.'

'They were thinking of somebody else. Anyway, Trends wasn't the only stint I did in subservience to my art. I've worked in old-clothes shops in the East End, in men's outfitters in the suburbs, in so-called salons in the provinces where they put one silk scarf and one Italian sweater in the window and sell trousers nobody would be seen dead in. I have even worked at an Irish draper's where the bar behind the shop was a lot bigger than the shop itself and far better patronised. That was over in the Republic. Besides all that, I've worked in Kensington High Street, in Oxford Street and (by virtue of knowing the management) in the clothing section of a Marks and Sparks. You name it, I've done it, so far as the sales side of the rag trade is concerned.'

'God bless my soul!'

'Keep on asking and perhaps He will.'

'It seems a lot of trouble to have gone to for a single book. That's what I meant,' I said.

'Ah, but what a book it's going to be! This is not a Rosie M. Banks, I'll tell you. I've had a hell of a time, sometimes hilarious, sometimes very unpleasant – occasionally, when walking home alone after dark in some parts of London, even quite dangerous – but I'm sure it will be worth it. I plan a monumental *opus* after the style of Dostoievsky. I ended up at Trends, packed the job in – couldn't stand the boss-lady for one thing – left my hotel and came to stay in this town with my sister and write the book. If you'd paid your sub to the lit. soc. as a gentleman should, and kept in with the rest of the crowd, you would have known I'd moved out of London.'

The gong went and we adjourned for lunch. The dining-room was full and, except for one mixed party at a central table which seated eight, all the guests except Imogen were men.

'I always try to pick a place which caters mostly for men,' she said, when we were seated, 'then I know I'm going to get enough to eat.'

'I always used to think you were on a perpetual diet. That's one reason why old Hara-kiri mistook you for Gloria when he took his wife to buy a dress at Trends.'

'*I* was called Gloria at Trends. Not my choice, needless to say. I inherited the name from my predecessor. As to my physique, I suppose I'm a *fausse maigre* like that girl in a novel by (I think) W.J. Locke. She looked like a starved cat in her clothes, but peeled to a goddess when she put on her swimsuit.'

'Ah!' I said. 'Splendid! When do I – ?'

'No lechery, please. I am convent bred,' she said, laughing. 'Now tell me *your* story.'

'Not here and not now. I intend to do full justice to this meal. Game soup and Southdown lamb – the local produce, I trust – don't go with murder and arson, so let me have my lunch and then you shall walk me round the town and I'll tell you all. Remind me, though, to send a telegram before we begin our peregrinations. I've got to scrub the false

131

information I enclosed in a letter to Dame Beatrice Lestrange Bradley.'

'Goodness me, you are flying high! Do you really write informative letters to Dame Beatrice? I met her once when she lectured to the lit. soc. on *Macbeth*.'

'I missed that. Yes, we are fellow sleuths. Get on with your soup or it will be cold. Everything shall be revealed when we are up on the Downs this afternoon.'

But I decided that it would be sacrilege to talk about burnt corpses while we were walking on the Downs so, as soon as I had sent off my telegram to the Stone House, I told Imogen all that I knew about Gloria Mundy as we explored the town.

We walked up the slope to the castle gatehouse and, as we were looking at what had been the outer bailey I said, 'I knew old Hara-kiri was mistaken.'

'About what?'

'He thought you were the ghost of Gloria Mundy.'

'Who is Hara-kiri?'

'Do you remember a vast man with a lot of yellow hair? I brought him to one of the lit. soc. dinners when my first book was published.'

'The man I called the Viking?'

'That's the chap.'

'But how could he have thought I was Gloria Mundy's ghost? That's the one and only time I ever saw him.'

'No. You saw him a few days ago in the Trends shop. He came with his wife to look at evening dresses.'

'But, Corin, I wasn't at Trends a few days ago. I left there weeks ago. That's why you didn't find me at that rather awful little guest-house. I was at Trends on a month's approbation and I left at the end of that month. I had got what I wanted and they had had enough of me. Don't look so moonstruck. Does it matter?'

'No. I suppose not. Strange, though, that the light-haired girl I spoke to thought I meant you and not Gloria Mundy.'

'I expect you asked for Gloria. We all had special names in that department. The light-haired girl you mentioned, and anybody who succeeded her in the job, was called Dorella. My number was five and all the fives would be known as Gloria and all the fours as Dorella and the third is always called Violetta and so on and so forth. Just an old Spanish custom at that particular shop.'

'But what an odd coincidence that you, of all people, should have been called Gloria.'

'Life drips with coincidences.'

'God bless them,' I said. 'Do you know something? An elderly disciple of Sprenger and Kramer told me I should meet you again.'

'You could have done that at the lit. soc.' There was a silence after this. I broke it.

'I ought to have tumbled to it, I suppose,' I said thoughtfully.

'Tumbled to what?'

I glanced at the fine dark-brown hair which a breeze was ruffling and replied, 'Brown hair, not really black. And you left Culvert Green almost a fortnight before the real Gloria would have done. That has rather upset my theories.'

'Oh, it was a bit of a dump, you know, and if you wanted a drink you had to go to the local. There wasn't even a table licence at the hotel. I used to get bottles from the off-licence and drink secretly in my bedroom. How on earth did you come to get mixed up in this murder business? How did it start?'

So I began at the beginning which, in a sense, was my meeting with McMaster outside Kilpeck church, for it was there I received my first report of Gloria Mundy, and told her the story.

'So there was really no connection between that and your meeting the actual girl at Beeches Lawn,' said Imogen. 'How strangely things work together!'

'Things don't always work together for good,' I said. 'In this case, they worked together for ill. I wish to heaven I had never gone to Beeches Lawn, especially now that I've mucked up my end of the enquiry.'

'But nobody asked you to make the enquiry, did they? Anyway, if you hadn't gone to Culvert Green we shouldn't now be heading for the ruins of a Cluniac priory.'

'I thought it was a Cistercian abbey.'

'Have it your way. Have you now told me all?'

'I think so. What do you make of it?'

'I'll answer that next time we meet, although goodness knows when that will be. Let's skip the ruins and go up on to the Downs. There are the remains of a hill fort and a couple of disc barrows up there. We can look at them and brood on the irrevocable past.'

'Is it so irrevocable?' I asked. She did not answer, so I went on, 'You can tell me nothing I don't know already about what is up on those hills. I've sub-edited a holiday booklet on this neighbourhood, don't forget.'

The Downs, as ever, were exhilarating, if that word can be used to describe anything so sublimely peaceful as 'here, where the blue air fills the great cup of the hills', and as we climbed towards the top of Firle Beacon there was one prospect which made me stop in my tracks. Away to the left the softly swelling contours took the shape of a woman's breasts. I said, looking at the hills and not at the girl beside me, something I had been longing to say to her years ago, but had been too poor, at that time, to offer her marriage.

'Will you have me, Imogen?'

'Yes,' she said, 'I'll have you, but I'm going to write my book first. You ought to have asked me ages ago. I always hoped you would. Am I the reason you stopped coming to the lit. soc. meetings?'

'Yes. I didn't have any money for marriage in those days.'

I booked dinner at the White Hart for the two of us and a room for myself for the night. I spent all next day with Imogen, lunched and dined with her again and then drove back to my flat under a hunter's moon. There was a heap of correspondence awaiting me. It included a letter from Dame Beatrice in answer to my telegram. She had written:

No, no, my dear Corin Stratford, I have a feeling that neither you nor Mr McMaster was wrong. I will attempt to supply chapter and verse in support of this theory and shall be very glad to know why you sent a telegram repudiating all your previous statements. Do telephone me when you have received this. As your telegram was not sent from London, I deduce that you are still on the trail, so I do not expect to hear from you immediately, but, please, when you have telephoned to say that you are at liberty, do come and see me as soon as you can and let me have all the latest news by word of mouth and face to face – so much more enjoyable and stimulating than a talk over the telephone or barren words couched in the restrained vocabulary of *littera scripta*.

Here there have been developments of a most satisfactory kind. I asked for and have obtained a full copy of the pathologist's report. It is most interesting and is one of two reasons for my thinking that the news you gave me in your letter bears the stamp of authenticity. The first reason is that, if Mr McMaster was ever in a state of such intimacy with Miss Mundy as he postulates, it is in the highest degree unlikely that he mistook another young woman for her at Trends. Ghost or no ghost, I am sure he saw Gloria Mundy days after she was thought to be dead.

As for the pathologist's report, as you will appreciate, forensic science has now reached such a stage of meticulous accuracy, due in large part to the work of Professor Keith Simpson and others, that the reconstruction of even the most maltreated corpse is not only possible but may be accepted without question.

In the case under review, the evidence is positive. Up to a point (which is to say it cannot tell us who the deceased was), it disposes of the myth that the body in the burnt-out house was that of Gloria Mundy.

You saw Gloria at Beeches Lawn and I am sure that you will endorse the views not only of Mr Wotton and his wife (asked separately for their opinion), but of William Underedge, Miss Brockworth, Miss Kay Shortwood and Mrs Coberley, with all of whom I have been in contact, that Miss Mundy was not more than about five feet five inches tall. The corpse, however, was well above that height before the fire charred off her feet. Moreover, the report gives an estimated age for the deceased of not fewer than sixty years. Is not science wonderful?

There was also a letter from Anthony Wotton. He wrote that he had telephoned my flat but had no answer. He supposed I was taking a holiday on the strength of the money I had received for the brochures and hoped I had not been spending all my time out on the tiles. When I got back, he and Celia would welcome it if I felt inclined to pay them another visit. There was a postscript:

Dame B has been here again and insisted on seeing Celia and me separately. When we compared notes afterwards, it seemed that she asked both of us to estimate the *height* of Gloria. Celia said that Gloria was at least two inches shorter than herself. I chanced naming an actual figure and put it at five five, which really comes to about the same thing, as Celia is five six and three-quarters.

I read this and then telephoned Dame Beatrice to say that I was back in London. She responded by saying that Coberley was up on remand in a day or two and that, in view of the evidence which was now available, there was much less chance of his ever being brought to trial unless the police could establish some connection between him and the so-far-unknown deceased.

'Of course,' she said in conclusion, 'the most telling evidence against him now is the fact that he knew where he had placed that impounded dagger, but I doubt whether it will amount to much. The broken window, which nobody disputes, means that some unauthorised person forced an entry, whereas Coberley had a key. Moreover, the dagger was in a wooden box which Coberley had made no attempt to hide – I believe you yourself saw the wooden box when he let you into the old house – and there is every probability that the intruder investigated the contents of the box. Whether the long dagger which Mr Coberley had placed in it was the weapon used to kill Miss Mundy's deputy I now have strong reason to doubt, as it appears to be beyond dispute that the murder was not committed at the old house or the body burnt there. When can you come to see me?'

'Is tomorrow too soon?' I asked. She answered that that would be splendid and that I was to get to the Stone House in time for lunch.

15
Little Progress

'Of course,' said Dame Beatrice when we met next day, 'one thing stands out clearly. Miss Mundy must have needed to have it supposed that she was dead. She took some risks to achieve this and at first it seemed that she had succeeded. The first thing which drew my attention to the facts was Miss Brockworth's assertion that the red and black scorched (but not burnt-up) hair was a wig. This could have been merely a spiteful remark from somebody who, quite obviously, disliked Miss Mundy, but when I challenged the police, the detective-inspector was compelled to admit that Miss Eglantine's possibly irresponsible statement was correct. The striking coiffure was indeed a wig and was the only means, so far as you and Mr Wotton were concerned, of identifying the body.'

'But of whom should Gloria have been so scared as to go to such lengths to fake a corpse to look like her own?' I asked.

'That has yet to be discovered. There could be two inferences, both of which will have to be examined. She may have feared that the police were on her trail for some crime she had committed earlier, or else she may have a personal enemy of whom she was desperately afraid.'

'Could be some relative of that Italian who committed suicide on Gloria's account,' I said, not really meaning my words to be taken seriously. Dame Beatrice, however, seized upon them.

'An Italian who committed suicide on Miss Mundy's account?' she said. 'Tell me about it.'

'I can't. I had the story at second hand and was given no details. I don't know how he killed himself or where or even when.'

138

'But there was some connection with Miss Mundy. From whom did you get the story?'

'I don't remember. I expect Wotton mentioned it. It would have come either from Wotton or McMaster. Nobody else I know would have spoken to me about Gloria. She must have been living with the Italian – he was an artist, it seems – and so got dragged into giving evidence.'

'There was no suggestion that it was anything but suicide, I suppose? But how should you know, since you had such a brief, undetailed account of it?'

'Are you wondering whether Gloria murdered the bloke?' I asked flatly.

'Well,' said Dame Beatrice, 'I do not rule out the possibility, since there seems a strong likelihood that she murdered that woman found in the old house at Beeches Lawn.'

'Well, if the police are of that opinion, it won't be long before they catch up with her.'

'London is a good place in which to hide.'

'She skipped from Trends pretty quickly when she realised that McMaster had recognised her.'

'That is dependent upon whether she *did* realise it, but let the inference stand. Do you know whether Mr McMaster has informed the police that he recognised her?'

'I don't know, but I'm pretty sure not. He's the kind of bloke who would always let the hen partridges fly.'

'Shades of Peachum, Mr Stratford?'

'I've just thought of something,' I went on. 'I've got myself a fiancée through this business and that fiancee may have been for a time on the staff of Trends while Gloria was there. Would you care to have a word with her? She herself was called Gloria, strangely enough, and the real Gloria would have been called by anything but her real name, it seems, but I have no idea what her shop name was. It could have been Violetta.'

'Is there any chance that your fiancee would have known Miss Mundy's address?'

'I should hardly think so. She was only at Trends to gather material for a book. I don't think she would have been in the least interested in the other assistants' private lives. I'll tell you who might be able to help, though. There is a silver-haired, pleasant young miss on the staff who knew more or less where my Imogen hung out during her stay at Trends, so she might be the best chance of our locating Gloria.'

'Well, we must not ignore any opening. Are you *persona grata* with this silver-haired young woman?'

'I don't know. I told her I was a policeman.'

'Enterprising of you, but perhaps, under the circumstances, not too helpful. People dislike what they call "getting mixed up with the police". I think perhaps it would be best if I myself made the next enquiries at the shop, but let us consider a few points before I do so. It is certain that Miss Mundy presented herself at Beeches Lawn on a Sunday, a day on which Trends would have been closed, but the evidence at our disposal suggests that she was also in the neighbourhood of Mr Wotton's residence on the Tuesday.'

'If McMaster is right in thinking that he saw her still working at Trends some time after that, she probably sent in a doctor's certificate to cover her absence, don't you think?'

'It seems a reasonable theory. On the other hand, if she had a car it would be quite possible for her to drive to Beeches Lawn directly she had finished work, do whatever she had decided to do there, and still get back to London and to the shop on the following morning.'

'A car? I don't know why, but I never thought of her having a car.'

'It is an ubiquitous possession nowadays.'

'Yes, of course. You don't mean she stole that car the police found outside the convent building, do you? – and burnt a body in it? Oh, no, that's far too fantastic.'

'That was a stolen car, according to the police theory, but, even if it had been her own, she still had to get back to London. Of course, there is always the train, but there is something more important than the fact that Miss Mundy does not appear to have given up her position at

140

Trends until after Mr McMaster's visit.'

'I still think there is just a chance he may have been mistaken. He saw a girl with black hair and a dead-white make-up. I believed I was convinced that he saw Gloria in this girl, but I find a lingering doubt,' I said. 'Would she have dared to go back to Trends, where she might be recognised?'

'We will shelve the point and go to another matter. Has it struck you that somebody, Miss Mundy or another, must have had that red and black wig in readiness and that the murder was premeditated and carefully planned?'

'I hadn't thought about it along those lines. That means all the murderer had to do was to find the right time to commit the crime.'

'And to select the right victim, of course.'

'The right victim? How do you mean?'

'She had to find a woman sufficiently of her own build, (although not necessarily of her own age), somebody who would be unsuspecting, and somebody who would not be missed for some time. Is there a picture forming in your mind?'

'Going on the assumption that Gloria Mundy knifed this so-far-unknown woman, burnt the body in that car and somehow – heaven knows how! – got the body back to the old house – well, if I can swallow all that, I can see various possibilities,' I said. This was not strictly true. What came into my mind were not possibilities, but wild flights of imagination into which, fortunately, perhaps, Dame Beatrice did not enquire.

She said, 'Let us pick up the threads again. Now then, we know that Miss Mundy was at Beeches Lawn on the Sunday. The host, the hostess and all the guests (yourself included) say so. Now what evidence have we that she did not leave the neighbourhood as soon as she had left Beeches Lawn after the soup incident?'

'Are you serious in asking that?'

'Please answer me.'

'Well, there is the evidence of Roland and Kay, who saw her standing at the window of the old house.'

'In pouring rain and gathering darkness, remember, and themselves,

I imagine, intent only on reaching the shelter of Mr Wotton's hospitable home.'

'But it wasn't raining, nor was the girl inside the old house, when McMaster saw her among the bushes as he crossed the kitchen garden. Of course he only saw the top of her head, I believe.'

'But it was, as you say, her head he saw, and her hair was, to him, unmistakable.'

'He didn't have the help of it at Trends.'

'Nevertheless, I believe him and I believe Mr Thornbury and Miss Shortwood. It was Miss Mundy they saw.'

'I thought you were doubtful about Kay and Roland.'

'Not if my interpretation of the known events is correct. I think the murder was committed on the *Saturday* night, the night *before* Miss Mundy presented herself at Beeches Lawn.'

'She would never have dared leave a stabbed and burnt body in that car. The police would have found it when the man who rented the old convent building reported the obstruction.'

'The car, I believe, was not drawn to their attention until the Monday or Tuesday.'

'That's true. They hadn't got rid of it even when Celia Wotton came back from the hospital after Miss Brockworth's accident. I suppose they were still trying to trace the owner, so wanted to have the car all in one piece, which it wouldn't have been, perhaps, if they'd moved it. Did Gloria steal the car as well as burn it.'

'No, I think it was her own car and an old one which she was prepared to sacrifice in order to further her own ends. The number plates, I am told – I have been in conference with Detective-Inspector Rouse, as you know – had been removed. My reading is that this was done to prevent the car's being traced to Miss Mundy, not that the vehicle had been stolen.'

'There are other ways of identifying cars, apart from their number plates,' I pointed out.

'No doubt she trusted that the fire would eliminate other clues. I will let you know how I get on at Trends. Where will you be during the next few days?'

'At Beeches Lawn, if I am not in my flat. The Wottons have invited me for another visit.'

The shell of the old house was a grim reminder of the days of my first visit to Beeches Lawn. What remained of the roof had been removed for reasons of safety, I supposed, so that, apart from the ravages which it had suffered from the fire, the house was now completely open to the weather. I wondered what Anthony proposed to do with it. I supposed that it was not impossible to renovate it, but in his place I would have pulled it down.

Celia opened the subject at lunchtime. She said that the house now gave her the horrors, but that Anthony wanted to preserve it. The contractor was coming that afternoon to make another survey.

'Now that the roof has gone, something must be done soon if I am to save the rest of the structure,' said Anthony, 'but Celia is too emphatic. The trouble is that, before I came into the property, a preservation order was slapped on the old place, so I've got to find out where I stand now with regard to that.'

'While Anthony and the man are confabulating, will you take me out in your car, Corin?' asked Celia. 'It's either that, or both of us staying indoors all the afternoon. I don't suppose the survey will be over until teatime at the earliest.'

'Where would you like to go?'

'Oh, anywhere. Just out and around. Anywhere you would care to take me.'

'Don't keep her out after dark. I don't trust bachelors,' said Anthony. I laughed as I thought of Imogen.

'I've got myself a girl of my own,' I said. Celia was all speculation and curiosity, but I said that, as the evenings were shortening and I had received my orders not to keep her out after dark, I would unburden myself to her uttermost satisfaction when we were in the car.

'Where are we going?' she asked, as I took the Cheltenham road.

'Can you climb a hill?'

'I hope so.'

'And visit a church?'

'If I have to.'

'Right. We'll climb up to Belas Knap and then go and look at Elkstone.'

I was surprised that she had never seen either, but then I remembered some American friends of mine who had been astonished to find how little I knew of historical London, a city in which I had spent the best part of my adult life.

I locked the car and we left the road and made the steep climb by way of a route marked out by the National Trust. A thousand feet up the shoulder of the beautifully named Cleeve Cloud was the long barrow, a grass-covered mound with an impressive forecourt, a false entrance and, round at the sides, the burial chambers in which, four thousand years ago, Neolithic men had buried the dead. I crept inside one of the short passages, but Celia remained outside.

'How did they make such a place?' she asked, when I emerged.

'Drystone walls made of limestone blocks,' I answered. 'The Cotswolds haven't changed.'

'*You've* changed,' she said, as we stood together in the wind which was driving ragged autumn clouds across the sky. 'Are you *very* happy, Corin?'

'As happy as a man contemplating matrimony can expect to be,' I replied. She laughed.

'A two-edged answer,' she said. 'Race you down the hill.'

'No, you won't. You'd find the slope too steep for safety. You'd tumble over and get covered in cowpats. I'm not going to have my car stinking like a midden.'

'Are you practising being a stern and bossy husband?'

I had a vision of Imogen with the gold lights in her dark hair and her answer to my proposal of marriage. 'I'll have you, but I'm going to write my book first.'

'Stern and bossy? I'd never get away with it,' I told Celia.

'It's old-fashioned, anyway,' she said. 'What's her name?'

'Imogen Parkstone.'

'Not the novelist?'

'Yes.'

'But I've read her! She's really good.'

'Is she? I don't read other people's novels for fear they are better than my own.'

'Does she earn a lot of money?'

'I've never thought about it. Maybe she does.'

'More money than you do?'

'Quite likely.'

'Will you mind if you find that she does?'

'No, it wouldn't make any difference. We should have an agreement to pay a certain amount into the housekeeping and keep the rest for ourselves, I suppose, to spend as we liked.'

'And take separate holidays?'

'That might come later.'

'I wish Anthony had never gone on that cruise. The knowledge that that awful girl is still alive haunts me.'

'Forget it. She is not likely to show up at Beeches Lawn again. Besides, Anthony got over that brief interlude of idiocy years ago.'

We found some blackberries in the lane, great luscious whoppers on bushes fertilised, I suppose, by the cows.

'Don't touch them,' said Celia, as I stretched out my hand for the fruit.

'Why not?'

'There's a country superstition that by this time in the year "the Devil's drawed 'is tail over 'em",' she told me, with a fair shot at the local intonation.

'Oh, ah?' I said, imitating it. 'So 'ow do 'ee come to know that there, then?' But I did not touch the blackberries. I thought of Aunt Eglantine and laughed as I unlocked the car. On the way to Elkstone I asked how Marigold Coberley was getting on.

'She is feeling much more hopeful,' said Celia. 'Mr McMaster wrote to her to tell her that he had seen Gloria Mundy alive and working at Trends.'

'Not her ghost?'

'No. He is convinced now that she is still in the flesh. The police are after her.'

We bypassed Cheltenham at Prestbury and followed the by-roads almost to Andoversford. Then I headed the car south-west to Seven Springs and after that it was due south to Elkstone.

The village was high up above the valley of the Churn and as harsh and uncompromising as the church itself. The edifice had been built roughly at the same time as Kilpeck, but, except for the chevron moulding around the broad chancel arch and an inner archway to the sanctuary, no two interiors could have been more different, neither were the south doorways comparable.

For one thing, both Celtic and Viking ornament were missing here. Elkstone was as brutal and as stern as the Normans who built it. There was Norman ruthlessness and cruelty in the hideous, warning sculptured faces at the crossing of the vault ribs of the chancel, and Norman thrift in the provision of a large dovecot under the roof, a dovecot which, when we had squeezed our way up a narrow stair, proved to be as large as the chancel below it.

When we were back in the car it occurred to me that we were so near Will Smith's cottage (as I still thought of it) that I might as well show it to Celia.

I guessed that my beloved lane would be knee-deep in wet vegetation and probably very muddy, but there was a made road up from the stables. These had been converted into classrooms and changing-rooms by the school, and some boys were just emerging as I left the car in the road. A young master was with them.

'Is it all right if we take this road to the gamekeeper's cottage? I used to know him,' I said.

'Oh, go ahead,' he responded; so we took the straight road to where the cottage stood at the top of the low hill. The slope was grassy and in front of the building Will had contrived a little unfenced garden, but this had run riot now and was covered in weeds. At the back were the woods where he and I had so often walked and talked.

Celia was enchanted with the cottage. I told her I wanted it for my own.

146

'Would you live here all the year round?' she asked. 'If so, you would need electric light and you would have to build a bathroom, wouldn't you? I would love to go inside.'

I began to demur, but then it occurred to me to try the back door, for country people seldom lock up. It did not yield, however, so we went round to the front, but that was fastened, too. I suppose the authorities did not want the property invaded by boys who wanted a quiet smoke.

'I expect we shall have to spend a lot of our time in London to keep in the literary fishpond,' I said in answer to Celia's question, 'but that will depend on Imogen.' I looked about me. On the sloping ground below, a drystone wall marked off a stretch of pasture and I remembered I had once seen a couple of bottle-fed lambs come bounding up to the farmer like pet dogs and there was still a grey mare in the paddock, although hardly the one on whose back I had been given a ride. 'For myself, I wouldn't care if I never saw London again,' I added.

'It's better for children to be brought up in the country. Are you planning to have a family, Corin?'

'Good heavens, we haven't got that far! Give us a chance,' I said. 'Anyway, at present, Imogen, I am sure, is far keener on producing books than children.'

16
Attempt at a Volte-Face

My activities following my return from Beeches Lawn to my flat were of no interest except to myself until I went to visit Miss Brockworth again. I took Imogen to look at Will Smith's cottage and outlined the improvements which would be needed if the school would let me have it. To my surprise she vetoed most of them.

'Electricity, yes,' she said. 'I expect they have it already in the village. I noticed a doctor's brass plate on that nice house as we turned into the lane; he is sure to have electric light. As for a bathroom and indoor sanitation, no. I am not going to spoil the character of the cottage like that. We will look about for an old-fashioned hip-bath, boil kettles of water over the fire and I will wash your back and you can wash mine.'

'Before or after we're married?'

'Don't be silly.'

'You won't like going to an outside privy in the snow,' I pointed out.

'We shall spend the summers here and the winters in London, so that question will not arise.'

I felt I had crossed the Rubicon and sold myself not to a pitched battle but into slavery. There was no going back. One good thing had happened while I was with the Wottons. I had met Marigold Coberley again and discovered that, greatly though I still admired it, her remarkable beauty made no emotional impact on me at all. In fact, studying her from what I hoped was an unprejudiced angle, I thought I could detect, in her wonderful eyes and her beautiful mouth, the ruthlessness which had led her to kill her first husband.

My effort at Trends and at Culvert Green had been fruitless so far as tracing Gloria was concerned, and, Imogen having retired to her sister's house to write, I found myself at a loose end and not in the right mental state to settle down to my own new book. Having time to kill, therefore, before the compulsion which all writers know came upon me again, I decided to go and visit Miss Brockworth, who was still immobile. I knew which were Celia's visiting days, so I was fairly certain that I could get the old lady to myself for an entertaining chat.

There was no doubt about her pleasure at seeing me and she received my package of peppermint creams and a perfume spray with approval. She then grinned wickedly at me.

'You have not come courting me, I hope,' she said. 'Chaucer's prioress is not for the marriage market, even though she be called madame.'

'Dear Madame Eglantine, I wish I had thought of you in time,' I said, 'but, alas and alack! – I am bespoke.'

' "And a tailor might scratch her where'er she did itch",' said the reprobate old lady, with hearty laughter. So, when she quietened down, I told her about Imogen.

'Is she good enough for you?' she asked.

'Much too good.'

'Well, I would trust you to pick out a sound apple from a basket of bruised ones,' she said. 'I should like to meet your Imogen. Did I tell you I had a visit from a priest yesterday?'

'Good heavens! You mustn't indulge in these morbid fancies. You're as sound as a bell.'

'Oh,' she said, 'I didn't *send* for him. He came of his own accord to ask me some questions I couldn't answer. They were about his brother who was supposed to have committed suicide a year or two ago.'

'Not an Italian?'

'Yes, of course an Italian. What a volatile people they are! And so disorganised.'

'I wonder why he came to see you? You didn't know this man who committed suicide, did you? – or know that it was because of Miss Mundy?'

'Certainly not. I should not dream of knowing the type of person who commits suicide. Apart from its being extremely wicked, it is in mighty poor taste. It gives the impression that one thinks it *matters* whether one lives or dies.'

'I suppose it matters to the individual concerned, but what did this priest have to say?'

'He said he was the brother of an artist whom the witch took up with and then murdered.'

'Suicide, not murder.'

'I know better and so does the priest. Tell me more about this Imogen of yours. When do you intend to marry her?'

So we abandoned the subject of the Italian priest and the remainder of my visit was passed in questions and answers about Imogen and authors' clubs and literary societies. I also gave her a description of Will Smith's cottage, which I hoped to purchase or rent from the school. On my way out I met one of the doctors.

'I wonder,' I said, 'whether you can confirm something the patient in there' – I gestured towards Eglantine's room – 'has just told me.'

'Oh, Granny Brockworth will say anything,' said the young man. 'Not that we dare call her Granny to her face. Sister tried it once to make her feel at home here, you know. She wanted to let the old lady feel that we would look after her, but she said that Sister had "impugned her honour and conferred on her a title of ignominy". She had never married, she told us, and certainly had never had children, let alone grandchildren. If she has said anything in complaint of her treatment here, you can disregard it, because it simply isn't true. She's a holy terror to the nurses, but she lacks for nothing in the way of care and attention, I can assure you.'

'It was nothing like that. She declares she has had a visit from an Italian priest and there are reasons why I would like to know whether that is true.'

'Dashed if I know. Patients' visitors are no concern of mine unless they upset the patient and I have to give orders that that particular visitor shall be discouraged from coming here. You had better see Sister if this priest was a nuisance.'

Sister was forthright.

'Her visitors have been yourself and, twice a week, her niece.

Nobody else has been. She seems rather friendless, and that's not surprising,' Sister said.

'The priest couldn't have slipped in without your knowledge?' I asked.

Sister froze me with a glare which would have turned Medusa herself to stone. I apologised and made my way out, wondering what story old Eglantine had got hold of and how she had come to know about the suicide at all. I discounted her claim that it had been murder. The verdict must have been clearly given at the time and had gone unquestioned ever since, so far as I knew. I decided to go back to Beeches Lawn to find out how Aunt Eglantine had come by her knowledge of the suicide.

'I go twice every week to the hospital,' said Celia, 'and it's difficult to keep finding fresh subjects of conversation, so we mostly talk about Gloria. I must have told her about the artist and I suppose she pondered over the story and has added to it. I suppose she gets bored in that room alone, and makes up fairy tales to amuse herself.'

'So Aunt Eglantine had the story from you and embroidered it.'

'And I had it from Anthony and he had it from the newspapers.'

'And there was no question of murder?' I asked Anthony.

'Good Lord, no! If there had been, I'm sure the boot would have been on the other foot and the artist chap would have murdered Gloria, not vice versa.'

'All the same,' I said, 'suppose some new evidence has come to light? Such things are not unknown. Suppose it *was* murder and Gloria had reason to believe that she would be involved? Wouldn't that be sufficient reason for her to have wanted it to be assumed that she was dead and that it was her body which was found among the ashes of the old house?'

'Trust a writer to build up a story! The constructive brain is never at rest,' said Anthony. 'Still, the hue and cry has gone out for Gloria, so all we can do now is to wait upon events and hope that the police will soon drop the case against Coberley. If Gloria is alive, there cannot be a case for him to answer.'

'Of course, the case against Gloria,' I said, 'rests solely on the substitution of that red and black wig for the victim's own hair.'

'What more do you want in the way of evidence, man? The sooner they find and convict Gloria, the better.'

From that moment I committed myself, rightly or wrongly, to Gloria Mundy's cause. My reason for doing so I still cannot explain. It was instinctive, reactionary and, on the face of it, absurd. I suppose Anthony's attitude irritated me.

I began to think of all the things there could be in Gloria's favour. We had no proof that, after her tempestuous leaving of the table at lunch that day, she had remained on Anthony's premises. It was true that Roland Thornbury claimed to have seen her at the window of the old house, but he could have been deceived. He had met her so briefly at Beeches Lawn that his identification of her rested largely, possibly solely, on her extraordinary bi-coloured hair, and, as we now knew, that could be counterfeited by a wig. It was also true that McMaster claimed to have seen her in the grounds and he, unlike Roland, knew her well and was not likely to have mistaken a stranger for her, particularly as the stranger, in other words the burnt-up corpse, had been so much taller than the real Gloria. All the same, he had seen little of her except the top of her head.

I put these thoughts aside and turned my attention to Aunt Eglantine. She had lied about the visit of an Italian priest; therefore it was more than possible that she had lied about having met Gloria in the old house.

Whether it would be of any use whatsoever to get in touch with her again and try to find out whether she would be prepared to change her story, I did not know. I thought I would ask the advice of Dame Beatrice about that. All I got over the telephone, though, was a cackle of laughter and her sardonic good wishes for the success of my efforts.

Reading this as advice not to trust either Aunt Eglantine's moral sense or her memory, I went to see McMaster.

'Good Lord! Of course I saw her,' he said. 'I saw her as certainly as I saw her in that dress shop.'

'But you didn't speak to her on either occasion, did you?'

'What does that matter? You had not spoken to me when you

recognised me at Kilpeck church that day, yet you had no doubt, even from a back view, who it was. I only saw Gloria over the top of some bushes in Wotton's grounds, it's true, but I could not have been mistaken, I assure you.'

'But she didn't attempt to hide from you, did she?'

'My dear fellow, she was off like a surprised snake. One flicker and she was gone. That happened in Wotton's grounds and again in Trends. Look here, what *is* all this?'

'Only that I think somebody ought to play devil's advocate. As things are, Gloria Mundy stands in all our minds as the murderess of that bewigged woman who was found burnt and dead in the remains of the old house in the grounds of Beeches Lawn. I don't think the evidence is good enough, that's all.'

'But what more do you want? The woman was got up to impersonate Gloria. Right?'

'Quite right.'

'Well, who would have wanted an impersonation of Gloria except Gloria herself?'

'Somebody who wanted to murder Gloria a bit later on, perhaps. Once she was presumed dead and her remains supposed to be in the grave, nobody was going to bother what happened to her after that.'

'Then why not have killed her there and then at Beeches Lawn?'

'Because the murderer may have been known to have been on the premises at about the same time as Gloria was there.' As I said this, I could see what an insubstantial argument it was, but I let it stand, although I wanted to add a bit to it in an attempt to justify it. He forestalled me.

'Oh, dash it all, Corin,' he said. 'The murderer must have known that, with forensic medicine at its present high level of knowledge and skill and all the facilities it has for the scientific study of dead bodies and the injuries which they have suffered, the substitution of another body for that of Gloria was bound to be discovered. The fact that the head was unrecognisable, whereas the wig was only badly scorched, was such a significant clue that the experts were bound to be suspicious and to make the most thorough investigation.'

'Perhaps you've got something there,' I admitted.

'Of course I have. It comes back to the same thing. Gloria Mundy murdered that woman and chanced her arm that a mistake would be made in identifying the corpse, as, apparently, it was at first, but it's rectified now, so her hunch has not come off.'

There was no denying this. I thought of tackling Roland Thornbury again, but shelved this in favour of getting in touch with Kay Shortwood. I got her address from Celia and telephoned Kay to ask for an interview, suggesting that we might have dinner together somewhere.

'Not unless Roland comes, too,' she said primly. 'I don't go out with unattached men now that our engagement has been announced.'

'Fair enough,' I said. 'I'll bring my fiancée. Will that clear the decks? We'll make a foursome of it.'

It proved to be a very expensive outing, but I got a private session with Kay because Roland loved dancing and Kay was not up to his standard but Imogen was, and he took the floor with her not once but four times, and left the two of us to talk.

'I really shall have to polish up my ballroom stuff,' Kay said. 'I don't intend to let this sort of thing go on much longer. It's either that, or weaning Roland off dancing, and I don't think that would be a very wise move.'

'Better ballroom dancing in the warm than watching rugger matches in the cold,' I said, thinking of Celia and Kate. 'Look, Kay, we haven't got a lot of time. I want to talk about Gloria Mundy. You and Roland saw her that evening you ditched your car. You saw her at the window of the old house. Can you be sure it was Gloria you saw?'

'Of course.'

'Why of course?'

'Because we recognised her hair and, from all that has come out about the murdered woman wearing a wig, the wig couldn't have been put on her head until she was dead and the bonfire had done its work on the body.'

'You know, I ought to have realised, when the police took me to the mortuary, that they had something up their sleeves. They knew the red and black hair was a wig, but at that stage they were not giving anything away. They just wanted my reactions.'

'Do you think that at that point they suspected Gloria of murder?'

'I don't know, but they must have suspected that it was to some-body's advantage to have it thought that Gloria was dead.'

'To put a wig on an otherwise burnt-up corpse was rather a crude way of establishing that, wasn't it?'

'Granted. Look, now, if it's all the same to you, let us lay off the burnt corpses. They don't go with this supposedly festive set-up.'

'You don't care that when the police catch up with Gloria – and they are bound to be hot on her trail – she may be found guilty of murder?'

'But she *is* guilty of murder! You could see it in those horrible green eyes of hers. They were just like pieces of hard, green glass.'

' "Nymph, nymph, what are your beads?" ' I quoted ironically.

' "Green glass, goblin. Why do you stare at them?" ' she retorted. 'That's what I said, Corin. Her eyes were green glass. The others are coming back to the table. Roland,' she went on, as they seated themselves, 'Corin is trying to whitewash Gloria Mundy.'

'No, I'm not,' I said, 'but she did go back to her job, you know.'

'Needed the money, I suppose,' said Kay. Imogen and Roland sat out the next dance and during subsequent dances Kay and I did not renew the topic. Altogether I found it a wasted evening and I wished I had made it an outing only for Imogen and myself. She was of the same opinion and voiced it when we got back to her flat.

'What on earth made you invite those two shattering bores?' she asked. 'Don't tell me that Kay Shortwood has charms to soothe your savage breast.'

'I thought you enjoyed dancing with Roland,' I said. 'Sorry if I was wrong.'

'The dancing was fine.'

'Well, then?'

'His conversation, what there was of it, was all about himself, of whom he seems to think extremely highly. There was one item, though, which might interest you. You remember we spoke of Gloria Mundy? Well, he said he wondered what had brought Gloria, in the first place, to Anthony's house. Did she ever tell anybody at Beeches Lawn her reason for calling there?'

'She definitely spoke to Anthony, but I'm not sure exactly what was said. My theory is that she was out of corn financially and had come to Anthony for help.'

'How long was she alone with him?'

'I can't say. I was up in my room working on McMaster's brochures. My guess is that Celia would have been present most of the time and, as it turned out, there was only that short interval before lunch when Gloria and Anthony could have got together and then, as I say, they probably wouldn't have been alone for long. Did they ever tell you at Trends why she left in such a hurry?'

'No, of course not. They couldn't, because I left weeks before she did. From what you've told me, I thought she left because Mr McMaster had recognised her.'

'Yes, I know, but, on thinking that one over, I am left wondering whether she *did* realise that he had recognised her. He thought it was her ghost he saw, if you remember what I've said.'

'All the same, she must have seen the effect her appearance had on him. She wouldn't have known that he thought she was a ghost.'

'I'm going to Trends to find out more.'

'They won't tell you more. They'll probably give you in charge for harassing them.'

'I shan't harass them. I shall only ask for more details as to why Gloria left. What do I call her? Was her "shop" name Violetta?'

'Yes, if she's the black-haired, green-eyed little bitch I think you mean. The other girls detested her.'

'I wonder what reason she gave for leaving?'

'What happened, I expect, was what I thought you had been thinking all the time. Gloria walked out on them when she realised that Mr McMaster had recognised her. From her point of view, the moment that happened the fat was in the fire. She must have been scared stiff anyway, when the autopsy was made public. She couldn't have given her right name when she signed on at Trends, though.'

'I suppose that she thought her completely black hair and a

dead-pan white make-up were sufficient disguise if anybody turned up at the shop who was acquainted with her, but, to anybody who knew her as well as McMaster had done, they proved insufficient and the detailed autopsy report proved, as you say, that the corpse couldn't be hers. I wonder whether it was Dame Beatrice who insisted on all those measurements and the rest of it?'

I received short shrift at Trends from the magnificent blonde. The day after McMaster's visit (she remembered him well, for not only was he a memorable figure, but apparently he had pulled himself together after he thought he had seen Gloria's ghost, and had lashed out as a big spender on dresses for Kate). Gloria, she told me, referring to her by her shop name of Violetta, had been so insolent to a customer later that day that instant dismissal had followed.

'Look, I've already been through all this with your lot, and I've read the papers. I cannot help you.'

'What did you gather from the papers?' I asked. She was impatient to get rid of me, but I was determined to have my say and ask my questions.

'What anybody who can put two and two together would gather. When she applied for a post here six years or so ago, her hair was a perfect sight, one half red – *not* a colour we encourage – and the other half black. The effect was most bizarre. However, she agreed to change it and the manager – a man, of course! – thought she had an engaging personality and would make a good saleswoman and her references (forged, I daresay, and, most mistakenly, not thoroughly investigated) were satisfactory, I suppose, so she obtained employment here.'

'Just one more question, if you will be so good,' I said. She tossed the blonde coiffure and told me that she supposed it was unwise to obstruct the police, but would I make it short, as she had already lost a customer to her second in command.

'Were you surprised that Violetta, as you called her, was so rude to a customer as to get herself dismissed?'

'Not altogether. The customer was a woman. The customers who come here are usually accompanied by gentlemen, and to gentlemen

Violetta was the best saleswoman I had.'

'I bet she was!' I said, thinking of those usually sane and sober men, Anthony Wotton and Hardie Keir McMaster. I realised, when I had settled down again in my flat and was trying to persuade myself that it was a good time to get busy on my own work, that something had shaken itself out of my subconscious mind and was clamouring for attention.

I don't know what had triggered off my new train of thought. Possibly I was somewhat frustrated that I could not use the Earls Court Road story about the murdered American woman, because it was too soon after that young woman had been stabbed and thrown into the sea. Apparently the murderer had never been traced and no doubt the case was still on the police files. They might not take kindly to somebody fictionalising it, I thought, and so inadvertently giving away clues.

Anyway, as I sat there at my writing-table trying to rough out a very different plot, the Earls Court and Hastings story came back to me and, although I could do nothing with it at that time in the way of turning it into a book, it got between me and my powers of invention and held me mentally a prisoner.

So I wrote to Dame Beatrice about it and at the end of the letter I put a large question mark and beside it I wrote Gloria's name. It took me a long time and several drafts before I was satisfied with what I had written, but at midnight I went out and posted it.

17
A Letter from Dame Beatrice

Dame Beatrice's answer came a few days later. She wrote that, acting upon what I had written, together with what she had already known or had surmised, she had been very busy. The rest of her letter bore this out. She seemed to have accomplished a very great deal in a very short time. She wrote:

When I received your letter Laura and I turned out our collection of cuttings and found details of the Earls Court case. The regular letters and postal orders which the deceased had received hinted plainly at blackmail. This was also the opinion of the police.

I visited the landlady, but she could tell me nothing useful except that among the dead woman's effects had been an expensive camera. From what your letter told me, I formed a theory that this could have been the camera with which the compromising photograph of Mr Wotton, Miss Mundy and the baby had been taken.

The police impounded the camera and all other effects belonging to the murdered American woman and I am told that they made every possible effort to trace any relatives she may have had (apart, of course, from her child) either in this country or in America, but had no success until quite recently. The camera contained no film, so there was no help to be obtained from it.

Acting on your information, but without mentioning your name, I have interviewed Mr Wotton. I asked him point-blank whether Miss Mundy had come to Beeches Lawn that day in order to blackmail him. He knew that I had talked with Miss Brockworth and he appeared to take it for granted that *all* my theories, instead of only some of them, were based on what she had told me.

He was extremely frank. He said that Miss Mundy had made one or two attempts, early on, to blackmail him on the strength of the photograph, but he had told her that her threats were useless, since his father and (later on) his wife knew the whole story and believed his version of it. It was not true that either of them knew anything of the kind, but she appears to have believed him and he heard no more from her and was greatly surprised and discomfited when she turned up at Beeches Lawn.

Well, now, it seems that she came to *beg* for money, not to demand it with menaces. She told Mr Wotton that all she wanted was to get out of the country. She promised that, if he would help her on this one occasion, she would never trouble him again. He refused to assist her in any way and was taken aback when his wife invited her to stay to lunch.

What follows is part theory, part fact. The *fact* that the murdered American woman received regularly letters containing English postal orders, plus the *fact* that she was murdered, give rise to the *theory* that when she had taken back her baby from Miss Mundy, she also made off with the camera, promising to give it and the film back when the payments had reached a certain amount. I do not think she kept her word.

This, of course, I cannot prove, but the payments could not have been very large if they could be covered by a weekly postal order. However, either Miss Mundy grew tired of being so consistently bled, or else, the agreed sum having been reached (and over a period of years, remember), the woman persisted in her demands and did not release the camera and the film. At any rate, there is no doubt in my own mind that Miss Mundy enticed the woman into a meeting with her and then killed her.

The Earls Court landlady's story that she was lured by the promise of a post in a hotel sounds to me very unlikely. Far more likely, I think, is that Miss Mundy, when she sent her last remittance, one which she fully intended should be final, suggested a meeting and a full settlement so that the woman could return to America.

The landlady told me that she had often expressed a wish to do so.

That in meeting her victim she might be placing herself in great danger appears never to have occurred to the woman. I suppose she thought that, after years of unquestioning payments, Miss Mundy was as a lamb for the slaughter. The slaughterer, however, was the lamb.

The Metropolitan Police have not yet closed the file on the case, and by piecing together bits of evidence gathered on both sides of the Atlantic they were already on Miss Mundy's trail before the murder at Mr Wotton's old house took place, and I am sure she knew that she was in danger. However, she must have thought she was safe as soon as the body found in the old house was identified by you and by Mr Wotton as her own. Then came the shock of realising that Mr McMaster had recognised her as the black-haired, white-faced assistant at Trends when she had thought that her disguise was impenetrable to those who had known her in the past when she had that striking head of red and black hair.

Certain that Mr McMaster would make known his discovery to the police – which, from a mistaken sense of chivalry he appears not to have done – she lost no time in getting away from Trends, but the police are busy searching for her. As you point out in your letter, Mr McMaster's evidence would not have been necessary to prove that she is still alive. The detailed autopsy proved that the dead woman at Beeches Lawn could not have been Miss Mundy.

When I had gained what I could from Mr Wotton, from the police and from the landlady, I wanted to establish a connection between Miss Mundy and this body found in the old house. It is you, my dear Corin Stratford, not I, who connected the two murders, although the police, with their relentless perseverance and patience, would have reached the conclusion you came to. From the American end they have established that Miss Mundy and the murdered girl were cousins.

Much is now in Mr Coberley's favour. For one thing, although both murders were stabbings, his dagger could not have been used for the murder of the American woman. Another pointer is that neither woman was murdered in her own home, but was *decoyed* and then killed. These, however, are nothing more than straws blowing in the wind. It was the autopsy which gave the police a clear lead in the chase after Miss Mundy.

Once it was shown that you and Mr Wotton had been misled in your identification of the body, added to the number of witnesses who were able to swear that Miss Mundy had been at Beeches Lawn shortly before the discovery of the body which had been furnished with that red and black wig – what a mistake that was on Miss Mundy's part, as matters turned out, although one can appreciate the difficulty she was in, of course! She had to make the features of the corpse unrecognisable, while, at the same time, finding some means of making sure that the body would be accepted as her own.

Imogen was with me when I received the letter. I handed it to her when I had read it so far, and asked for her views and comments. When she handed the pages back, she said, 'I wonder whether the American girl was told that the whole business of the baby and the photograph was intended as a joke?'

'Likely enough she was talked into it that way, but she soon seems to have realised its possibilities so far as she herself was concerned. She must have been relying on Gloria to give her a home and get her a job and then found out, when she had kept her part of the bargain and taken the photograph, that Gloria was going to ditch her. The rest, it seems to me, follows on naturally.'

'Yes. Without the photograph, Gloria was in no position to put pressure on Anthony Wotton, although it seems she did try to call his bluff once or twice. When, in the end, she went to Beeches Lawn, it looks as though she managed to get a short private talk with him, doesn't it?'

'And that, I think, is where my naughty old Madame Eglantine comes in. I have no doubt she was intrigued by the visitor, speculated upon the purpose of the unheralded visit, listened behind the door and collected an earful of what may be termed 'baby-talk'. She doesn't like Anthony, so she told the tale to me and possibly to others.'

'She really is a dreadful old thing. Why do you like her?'

'She's amusing and stimulating, if only you can keep her off the *Malleus*; but, to go back to Dame B's letter, it's now clear why Gloria wanted money from Anthony to get herself out of the country before the net closed in on her. The police were hot enough on her trail – must have been, you know – to cause her to fake her own death.'

'And in case Anthony refused to sub up, all *that* had been worked out before she ever went to Beeches Lawn. I wonder how she managed to find a victim who, apparently, would never be missed.'

'Perhaps the rest of Dame Beatrice's letter will supply the answer to that. All the same, London must be full of people who wouldn't be missed – lonely spinsters, friendless widows, people who have been in gaol and are living under assumed names, immigrants who haven't yet put down any roots. It would be easy enough to find somebody about whom there would be no hue and cry.'

'Your picture, although touching, is not convincing,' said Imogen. She handed Dame Beatrice's letter back to me and I read the rest of it, but, before I did so, I said, 'I wonder what happened to that roll of film with Anthony, Gloria and the baby on it?'

'I expect the girl turned it over to Gloria when she received the promise of full payment.'

'She probably received the payment but Gloria took it back after she had killed her.' We read on:

My next visit was to Trends. I went armed with my full credentials and applied not to the department you and Mr McMaster visited, but to the office, where I asked to see the manager.

A suave individual took me into his own small sanctum and sent his secretary to bring us coffee. When she had gone for this, he asked me whether his firm was in any trouble, as he knew of no circumstances which could lead to a visit from a representative of the Home Office. I reassured him and added that I was interested in

163

one matter only. I was anxious to know whether any elderly woman on his staff had retired during the past few weeks.

He mentioned the summary dismissal of Miss Mundy, to whom he referred under another name, but not her shop-floor title of Violetta, and admitted he had already been questioned by the police as to her whereabouts but he added that she was anything but elderly. I mentioned that the age I had in mind was round about sixty. He could not help me, but when the secretary came back with the coffee he sent her out again with instructions to ask Personnel to spare him a few moments.

A grey-haired, pleasant, but businesslike woman appeared and to her I put my question. She replied that one of the cleaners who had reached what she termed 'senior citizen status' had retired within the past few weeks and that Personnel had enquired about her future prospects and had asked whether she would be able to manage on the state pension.

The answer was satisfactory, she thought. One of the girls in the gowns department had promised to get her work as a cleaner in a block of flats where a trustworthy charwoman was required, as most of the tenants were out at work all day, so that the cleaner would be given keys and would be alone in the various apartments. The personnel officer could not supply the address of the flats, but she gave me the cleaner's own address, which, of course, she had on her books.

I have given this address to the police, but first I visited the place myself. It turned out to be a council flat in a large block. The cleaner had occupied a bed-sitting room in the home of a middle-aged, respectable couple who lived in Wapping. She had told them that she had found part-time employment which necessitated her giving up her room in their flat, but had left no address 'as she never got any letters, anyway,' and they 'could do with the extra room', so I could not follow up my enquiries. No doubt the police will do better and I shall be very much surprised if this cleaner does not turn out to be the victim found in Mr Wotton's old house. Gloria would have found out all about the poor, friendless thing.

'Well, that seems to tie that up very neatly,' said Imogen. 'When am I going to meet your Dame Beatrice?'

'Soon, I hope. I'm not sure which of my old ladies I love more, her or Madame Eglantine.'

18
Exit Gloria

It seemed to me that there was nothing more that I could do. My foolish impulse to attempt to whitewash a double murderess had vanished long before I received Dame Beatrice's letter and there appeared only two minor points to be cleared up, neither of them my business. The ownership of the burnt-out car had not been established and nobody so far had suggested how the elderly cleaner's charred and disfigured body had been conveyed to the old house.

I put these points to Dame Beatrice in another letter and she in her reply invited me to bring Imogen to stay for a weekend at the Stone House. Imogen, who was staying with her sister and finding the children charming but distracting, responded warmly to the invitation, so on a cold autumn Friday afternoon we drove to the New Forest.

I had met the children when I picked Imogen up at her sister's house and, as we were leaving the Downs behind us and I was taking the road to Chichester and then to Romsey to avoid Southampton, she mentioned that she would have to move, in order to get enough peace in which to write her book; I suggested that her next move should be into my pad.

'Then, as soon as the winter is over, we'll go house-hunting in London and in the summer we'll move into the Cotswold cottage,' I said.

'Marriage lines or no marriage lines?'

'We might as well regularise the union, I suppose,' I said, as I kissed her cheek.

'Thank you,' she said. 'That remark might have been more happily phrased, but it indicates honourable intentions. Make it before

Christmas and then I shan't need to join in the family festivities.'

'I've never made love to you properly,' I said thoughtfully. 'When do I repair the omission?'

'Well, it would be most improper to do it under Dame Beatrice's roof,' she answered with mocking primness.

'She would only cackle and wish us well. Do a few lines on a bit of paper matter so much?'

'Yes, if they mean that you have to maintain me in sickness and in health, whether you like it or not.'

'Oh, Lord! Not a church wedding?'

'With you complete in sponge-bag trousers and a buttonhole. Besides, just in case you thought differently, I am entitled to be married in white.'

'I've never thought about it. I have to confess that I myself am a spotted and inconstant man.'

'Just as well that one of us has had some experience.'

'This is the most unromantic conversation I ever took part in!'

'It is nothing to the boring dialogues we shall have when we are married.'

'Then there's no time like the present.' I pulled into a lay-by which fortunately was empty.

Breathless at the end of the next ten minutes, she said, 'Perhaps it won't be so boring after all. Where did you learn your technique?'

'Not from Gloria Mundy,' I said.

'Stop at Romsey Abbey. There's a stone carving outside the south door,' she said. It was a crucifix. Unbidden to my mind came the Celtic warrior at Kilpeck. I banished his image and gently took Imogen's hand. The figure on the crucifix was not quite life-size, but, unlike most such portrayals, the eyes were open and the head was raised. It was a representation of *Christus Dominans* and may have been brought back from the Middle East by crusaders, or so I had read. It seemed very likely, for the figure was too anatomically correct to be of Saxon origin, as some claimed, and it was a figure of victory, not of death.

'This place was built for a convent of nuns,' I said, as we walked back to the car.

'And the carving was outside the abbess's door,' remarked Imogen. Nothing more was said until we reached Lyndhurst and even then all I said was, 'Not far now.'

It was growing dusk. The road between Lyndhurst and Brockenhurst is one of the most beautiful major routes through the New Forest and in the dim evening light the majestic trees gave cathedral solemnity to the scene. I drove slowly and we did not talk.

Once over the little river, the Stone House soon came into view. Dame Beatrice and Laura Gavin received us kindly, George, the chauffeur and general handyman, carried our suitcases upstairs and Laura and Imogen followed so that Laura could show Imogen our rooms. I was left downstairs with Dame Beatrice.

'We are going to be married sooner than I thought,' I said.

'The sooner the better,' she responded, 'once minds are made up. Has Imogen parents living?'

'No. I expect she will be married from her sister's house. As for me, I expect old Hara-kiri will arrange to put me up the night before. He doesn't live all that far from where she will be.'

The next two days were crisp and cold. Imogen and I walked in the forest, chaperoned by Laura's two mighty Dobermanns, and returned to eat Lucullan meals prepared by Henri, the French cook, and served by Celestine, his wife, who regarded Imogen and me with a dewy, sentimental eye and on one occasion said, 'Ah, the poor children! What suffering comes after *les noces*!'

When we had left the Stone House I went to visit Aunt Eglantine to tell her of my approaching nuptials.

'I suppose you'll expect a wedding present,' she said.

'The best one would be your good wishes, dear Madame Eglantine.'

'Don't talk such abysmal nonsense!' she said. 'Promised you millions, didn't I?'

'An embarrassment of riches and one with which I could not cope. Make me another of your prophesies.'

'I am no prophetess. I speak only of the things I know.'

'Such as?'

'Such as that I buttered the schoolmaster's steps and I sent the letter to him pointing the finger at the witch.'

'*You*? But you might have killed Mrs Coberley?'

'She is a murderess, isn't she?'

'You have no right to say that. She was acquitted.'

'Be that as it may, men always are fools when they meet beauty face to face. Look at Helen of Troy.'

'I wish I could.'

'There you are, you see. And you about to be married to this blue-stocking of yours!'

'She isn't a blue-stocking.'

'When am I going to meet her?'

'I don't know that you are. I don't trust you with anything I hold precious. Did you really butter those steps?'

'What do you think? I wanted to find out whether she was another witch. If she had not tumbled down the steps I should have known her for one. She had saved herself from life imprisonment, so I thought she could save herself from a nasty little fall.'

'I shall never forgive you.'

'Then I shan't tell you how the black witch took the body to the old house.'

'You don't know that.'

'I worked it out. She came in a car, didn't she? She burnt the car. She borrowed another one.'

'How could she do that?'

'Anthony Wotton has only one double and one single garage. The other cars were left outside. People are careless. They don't always lock their cars. They think that at the houses of friends they are safe.'

'You may be right about that. Over that weekend there would have been – let's see. Ah, yes. Anthony's car and Celia's mini in the double garage, and mine, as I was the first guest, in the car-port. That means that Roland Thornbury's car, William Underedge's, Dame Beatrice's and, for the night he was there, Hardie McMaster's, were left in the open.'

'Not Roland Thornbury's. It was bogged down,' Aunt Eglantine reminded me. 'And the white witch had gone.'

'But, supposing that you are right and that's the way she got the body from the burnt-out car to the old house, how did she hide it from the Saturday night until the morning the gardener found it?'

'I worked that out, too,' said Aunt Eglantine with great satisfaction. 'I've had nothing to do here but quarrel with the nurses and think my own thoughts. She killed that woman on the way down here and put the body in the boot before she set fire to the car. All she had to do was to go to a hotel in the town – you will never know which one because she will have given a false name and it's not a thing which matters –'

'It matters if it proves that she was actually in Hilcombury on that Saturday night. She didn't show up at Beeches Lawn until the Sunday.'

'Very well.' Aunt Eglantine closed her eyes. 'That's all,' she said. 'She couldn't move the body to the old house until the car had cooled down.'

'Even so, when did she get a chance to move the body without anybody knowing?'

'It gets dark early at this time of year. All Anthony Wotton's people would have been indoors and his gardeners would have gone home. It would have been easy enough for her. An ordinary person might have run into trouble, but not a wicked black witch like her.'

'Your thinking seems to have been deep, logical and constructive, clever old Eglantine. You have an answer to everything.'

'Oh, people think I'm crazy,' she said, opening her eyes, 'but I can out-think most of them when I put my mind to it. Anyhow, I've told the police all that I've told you and they believe me, even if you don't. They'll catch up with her, you mark my words.'

'Are you telling me that she risked staying in a local hotel all those nights after she had burnt the car with the body in it?

'I don't know. She was in the old house for part of the time. She was seen by others and I met her there when I had my accident.' She chuckled. 'She wasn't expecting any of us, I'll wager,' she said, 'neither those young people who got caught in the rain or me so early in the morning.'

I thought of the empty cans of food and drink which had led to Rouse's enquiries about squatters. Her explanations could have covered those, too. Hotels are expensive nowadays.

'She would have been pretty cold in the old house,' I said. Aunt Eglantine had an answer to that.

'Not if she chanced the staircase and made a fire in one of the bedrooms,' she said. 'The stairs would have borne a lightweight like her, I daresay, whereas I brought them crashing down.'

'Smoke from a bedroom fire, or anywhere else in the old house, would have been noticed,' I pointed out.

'Well, it wasn't. It took a conflagration to draw attention to the old house, didn't it? Do stop raising silly objections. All that I've told you covers the known facts, so have done with your contumacious carpings, young man.'

I returned to my flat and tried to settle down to work, but it was impossible to concentrate on the new book. What with the conversation with Aunt Eglantine and my approaching marriage, I found myself incapable of serious application to creative writing. I soon gave up the attempt and wrote to Imogen instead. That is to say I was halfway through the letter when Anthony's call distracted me. He sounded incoherent.

'Stop!' I said. 'Take a deep breath and begin again. Are you tight?'

Apparently he relinquished the phone to Celia, for it was her voice which came through.

'It's that girl again,' she said. 'Do come.'

'Has she been arrested?'

'No, and Cranford Coberley is free. Drop everything and come, please. We need you badly.'

I did as she asked. I left my letter unfinished, got my car and drove straight to Beeches Lawn, stopping only to pick up a sandwich and some coffee on the M4. When I had pulled up in the forecourt of Anthony's garage, I locked the car, a precaution I had never taken before at his place, and as I walked by the kitchen garden I met Platt, the gardener.

'Beg pardon, sir,' he said, 'but, in case you didn't know, there's trouble up at the house.'

'Yes, I had a telephone call,' I said.

'That's all right then, sir. You won't be getting a shock.'

I did not ask him to explain what the nature of the shock would have been. I knew that Anthony and Celia were alive and that was all that concerned me at the moment. I hurried along to the house. Celia opened the front door.

'The servants are having hysterics and Anthony isn't much better,' she said. 'Come in and have a drink. We can all do with one.'

She took me into the enormous drawing room. Anthony was at the window staring out at the almost leafless trees. He turned round as we came in.

'Hullo, Corin,' he said. 'Good of you to come. We're in trouble again.'

Celia went out and returned from the dining-room next door with bottles and glasses.

'I met your gardener,' I said. 'What's happened now? Not Aunt Eglantine, I hope?'

'Oh, no, it's Gloria Mundy. She's dead,' said Celia. 'The servants found her lying outside the back door. The police have been here again and so I suppose all hell will be let loose once more. Will that wretched girl never stop causing trouble? Help yourself, Corin, and don't stint.'

I poured drinks for all of us. Anthony was almost too shaken up to hold his glass. I wondered whether he had gone on caring for Gloria after all, or even whether he had killed her.

'So what happened?' I asked.

'We don't know. The servants came in just as we were finishing breakfast and blurted out the news, so Anthony went out there. She was quite dead. Of course the police had to be told and Detective-Inspector Rouse came again. He is becoming quite an old friend,' said Celia bitterly. 'He badgered us and the servants with questions and then had the body taken away. We could tell him nothing, of course, and we don't know where we stand. It really is unutterably awful.' Her calm demeanour suddenly crumpled. She burst into tears. This pulled Anthony together. He took the glass from her hand, laid it very precisely on the side table and collected her on to his lap. At the same moment the doorbell pealed.

'I'll go,' I said; but the maid also had pulled herself together sufficiently to answer the door. She let in Rouse. I met him in the little vestibule and took him along to the drawing-room. I gave a loud knock on the door to suggest to the others that they had better unscramble themselves.

They were in separate chairs when we went in and, although Celia's cheeks were flushed, her eyes were dry.

'You are just in time for a drink, Detective-Inspector,' she said.

'No, thank you, madam. I shan't keep you a moment. There will have to be an inquest, of course, but we found a letter on the body. It will be handed to the coroner in due course, but it is addressed to Mr Wotton, so I think he had better read it.'

Anthony took the envelope and unfolded the letter which was inside it. He perused it and then handed it to me. There was no doubt about its being a suicide note. In it Gloria said that she knew the game was up, that she had no intention of spending years in prison, that she regretted the death of the elderly cleaner, but not the murder of the American cousin – 'she only came over here to sponge on me because she thought I was still Hardie McMaster's mistress and he is a very rich man' – and the letter went on to mention the photograph 'with which I never intended any harm, but only something to hold, Tony, over your rather stupid head, but she went off with it and I did my best to buy it back so that she could do you no harm with it. Tony, my weak-kneed old darling, if your gardener must keep all that lethal stuff in his shed, he should keep it locked up. There is enough poison in there to lay out a regiment.'

She named some of the substances. All of them, I knew, contained hydrocyanic acid, more commonly known as prussic acid. There would have been pesticides such as rat poison, wasp-killer and a fumigatory for trees and fruit. Which she had used she did not say. The letter ended:

> I have read somewhere that certain natives kill themselves on the doorstep of an enemy so that their ghost will haunt him. I bear *you* no malice, but I will haunt that bitch of a woman you married until she kills herself to get rid of me. She looked at me as though I was scum. Even that Coberley woman only laughed when the soup went over me. I can forgive her for that, but I won't stand being treated like dirt by that wife of yours.

I handed back the letter. He gave it to Rouse without showing it to Celia.

'I must ring up Hara-kiri,' he said, when the inspector had gone. 'I don't want him to hear about this from the newspapers. I wonder, Corin, whether you would do it for me? You'll do it better than I would, because you are in no way involved.'

'I'll ring him up from my flat, then,' I said. 'Now that you are out of trouble, I think the two of you are better on your own.'

The fact was that I was anxious to get away. There was nothing useful that I could do by staying and I was superstitious enough not to want the Wottons' bad luck to attach itself to me:

Back in my flat, I had a dream I shall not forget. I am well aware that nothing is so boring as having to listen to an account of someone else's dreams, but, because of Aunt Eglantine's strange and bizarre request later, this dream of mine still seems of peculiar significance. It began when I dreamed I received a 'Tag Map' from Hara-kiri.

19
A Kind of Pilgrimage

In my dream I was not only mystified; I was alarmed. A 'Tag Map' went back to our college days. It was a code which meant 'Time all good men aid party' and one was in honour bound (by an initiation oath taken in the Junior Common Room) to honour it. I remembered the row at Pontyprydd after the rugger match there and wondered in what fresh trouble and harassment Hara-kiri intended to involve me.

At first the dream was unco-ordinated and chaotic. I found myself outside his house, but it had changed. Instead of the modern homestead which he had built in the Sussex countryside, it was a replica, on a smaller scale, of the second of the Cornish hotels I had visited. There was the same mixture of architectural styles, from the mediaeval to the early Georgian, there was the grim gatehouse, and there was the tall turret with the little room at the top where I had slept. I found myself up there again and below me were the coast and the rocks and a tiny cove which had not been there before.

Hardie came into the room. I knew it was he, although some of the time I thought he was Anthony. He invited me to look over the house and took me into a room which I seemed to recognise, although in fact I had never been inside it. It was beautifully decorated and furnished and over the mantelpiece was Ruben's *Adoration of the Magi* which, in my dream, I knew to be the original, but it turned into the naked figure of Gloria Mundy and Aunt Eglantine laughed and said, 'The quickness of the hand deceives the eye,' before she turned into Hara-kiri again.

He said, 'She's in the room which used to be the chapel.'

'Aunt Eglantine?' I asked. However, it turned out to be Gloria, as I might have guessed. I thought of Kate and asked where she was.

He said, 'I have divorced her. Didn't I tell you? This is to be purely a stag party.'

'But I'm not going to be married for a good many weeks,' I said. 'What are the candles for?'

'A lyke-wake dirge. If you want to see Gloria, she is on the bed.'

I could see that we were now in a chapel. The windows were small and gave an ecclesiastical appearance to the room and the candles, six of them, were the only form of lighting. The only furniture was a four-poster bed on which lay a coffin with no lid. There in it lay Gloria, her black and red hair neatly arranged, her unprepossessing little face looking rather like that of Kay. There was a cat-like smile on her lips and her predatory hands were clasped together on her breast.

As I looked down on her I knew that one of the candles had gone out. I straightened up and lighted it with a snap of my fingers, but the little room went dark and I found myself in the courtyard in front of the house. Instead of Hardie's big car there was a hearse and behind it a smaller car with four men in it. I could not see their faces, but I knew that they were William Underedge, Cranford Coberley, Anthony and Anthony's gardener.

'We had to bring Platt,' said Hara-kiri, 'because we need an experienced man to do the digging.' At that I knew we were going to bury Gloria.

'*Requiescat in pace,*' I said under my breath.

McMaster either heard the words or guessed them correctly, for he said, 'Yes, but will she?'

'Will she what?'

'Rest in peace. Wotton doesn't think so. She is to be dealt with tonight. She threatened to haunt him. We can't allow that.'

'Surely you don't believe that sort of rubbish?' I said.

'I don't altogether disbelieve it. Anyway, I have everything ready, but we need your help.'

'To do what?'

'Well, never mind that now. We'll discuss it when the others turn up.'

'Others? But they are here, Anthony and the rest.'

'Anthony is bringing a young, tough chap named William Underedge. You and I met him at Beeches Lawn on the day the storm set in. There really ought to be six of us, but the fewer who know of this business the better. What shall we carve on the headstone?'

'You are at your old game of collecting epitaphs, then. Not in the best of taste on the present occasion, I would have thought,' I said with grave disapproval.

He took no notice. He took me along to his dining-room. There was food laid out and wine on the table.

'I've given the servants the evening off,' he said. Then he added, 'I'm serious, Corin, and your guess is perfectly correct. Don't you know some rhyme or other about six pall-bearers? Sit down and let's tuck in. We shall need our strength for this night's work.'

'Aren't we going to wait for the others?'

'No. They will have something on the road. Spout away.'

I told him that I thought I could oblige him with a couple of verses. I recited,

> ' "Tell me, thou bonny bird,
>   When shall I marry me?
>   When six braw gentlemen
>   Kirkward shall carry ye." '

He had brought a notebook to the table, but he did not use it. He wrote the lines on the table-cloth which I now realised had been Gloria's winding-sheet.

'Any more?' he asked. 'You said a couple.'

'The only other one I can think of concerns a man. It won't do for Gloria.'

'Perhaps it will do for me myself later on.'

'Hardie,' I said, 'did you really love that girl?'

'Difficult to remember. I suppose I must have done. But come! Your epitaph, for your question needs some excuse.'

'A very nice derangement of Shakespeare! All right, but I shall alter it a bit from the original. It's really a cowboy song, but, as you are a Scot, here goes:

> ' "Find six lusty clansmen to carry me kirkward,
> And six sonsie lassies to greet on my pall,
> And on my black coffin strew handfuls of heather
> To deaden the sound of the sods as they fall." '

'I wish there could have been six of us,' said McMaster, 'but she is only a lightweight, so perhaps we can manage.'

'There *are* six of us,' I said, and there we all were.

Anthony said to McMaster, 'Is everything ready?'

'Yes,' he replied. 'I cut and sharpened the stake of holly this morning and there is a box. It will be lighter to carry than the coffin. Besides, we mustn't risk damaging that. The other funeral is to be tomorrow and everything must be in order, because you are a churchwarden.'

Then we were back in the hearse. I had no idea where we were going. Anthony and Hardie had carried out a long narrow box with a fitted lid and I knew it had come from the room which had been a chapel. The box was put on to the back seat of Anthony's car. William Underedge squatted on the floor to keep the box from sliding off the seat and Hardie and I took the lead in the hearse with Coberley and the gardener sitting on the empty coffin.

It was when we got to Cirencester, with its unmistakable church porch, that I began to have some idea of what our destination was to be. As we headed for Cheltenham, Hardie said, 'Belas Knap is what we want. You'll have to guide me. In fact, you'd better drive.'

'Pull up,' said William Underedge, who suddenly appeared beside me. 'I want to change places. For one thing I'm stiff and cramped and for another I expect I know the route better than you do in the dark.' So they changed over and for the last few miles of the drive William and I were in charge of all that remained of Gloria Mundy, for she was in the coffin again.

Our progress was slower once we were on the byroads, but the journey was finished at last. We waited for Anthony to pull in behind us and then he and McMaster lifted, not the coffin, after all, but the long box, out of Anthony's car and we began the steep climb up the shoulder of Cleeve Cloud. The moon had risen and the cold night was clear.

Anthony and Hardie carried the box, occasionally relieved by William and myself. Coberley and the gardener followed behind with spade and pickaxe. We slipped and stumbled. I thought of the cowpats and hoped I would not measure my length among them. Hardie swore now and then, but Anthony and William plodded on. I thought of some caving I had done in Derbyshire, and of how I was once lost in the Sahara. I have explored caverns in the Carpathians and I have visited the Callanish stones at midnight on Midsummer Eve, but I have never made so extraordinary a journey as on the long and difficult ascent of Cleeve Cloud in my dream. For every step we took upwards we seemed to slip back two.

The moon, bereft nowadays of all its mystery, gazed blandly down on us and then suddenly above us loomed the great mass of Belas Knap. As we reached the skyline, the wind, from which we had been sheltered on our side of the hill, struck us with its full force and we had to hold on to the box to prevent it from blowing away, for I knew that, even with Gloria inside it again, it weighed no more than a piece of paper.

We were now standing in front of the false portal with its two upright blocks of stone, with their lintel top. The massive boulder which appeared to be the door only served to conceal the fact that an entrance did not exist on this, the highest and widest part of the mound. The openings were all in the sides. (Here my dream played no tricks.)

The wind dropped and the bearers laid the box down. Hardie removed the lid. The body was covered by a folded sheet. Hardie took this out, spread it on the ground and then he and Anthony took up the frail corpse and laid it carefully on to the sheet. In the moonlight the meagre features looked grey and disquietingly old. The red hair seemed to have lost its colour, but the black locks lay like soot against

179

the grey face. Clumsily, and yet with tenderness, Hardie, who was still on his knees, bent forward and stroked the hair back a little. Then he stood up and said, 'Well, this is it.' He took from his pocket a short piece of sharpened stick. William shone his torch on it and I saw that it had been freshly cut from a living plant and was bleeding.

'You'll want a piece of stone,' said Anthony, 'to bash it in.'

'No. I've brought a mallet. Make a quicker and better job,' said William. I now noticed that he had a hessian bag slung over his shoulder. 'There ought to be crossroads,' he muttered.

'You or me?' asked Hardie of Anthony.

'You,' said Anthony. He knelt and carefully pulled up the ridged sweater and uncovered the pitiful little breasts. Hardie knelt on the other side of the body, placed the sharpened end of the short stake over the heart and struck the holly branch one sharp blow. There was silence. The two men remained where they were. Then Anthony said, 'Goodbye, Gloria. Don't come back, there's a good girl.' McMaster pulled down the sweater, but I saw that it had turned into the Kilpeck warrior's byrnie of leather and chain mail.

'We ought to put her in with the others, you know,' said Anthony.

I took the torch and made my way round the side of the limestone-built, turf-covered burial place and entered the first of the chambers. It was a short passage rounded out at the end. It was bitterly cold in there and I imagined it still had the smell of death on it from the corpses which had lain in it four thousand years before. When I got back to the others, Gloria was back in her box and the others were sitting on the lid. They rose, we formed up like bearers, three on either side of the box, and bore it towards the passage I had entered.

'This is number thirty-seven,' said William Underedge. 'Make her welcome. She is very cold.'

I struggled out of my dream and found that all my bed-coverings were on the floor and also that a sashcord had parted and the window was wide open.

I went to visit Aunt Eglantine on my way back to my flat next day.

'I want you to buy me a doll,' she said. I laughed and told her that a

Teddy bear would be more companionable and more cuddly. 'No,' she said, 'I fancy a doll. A rag doll would be best, but I doubt whether they make such things nowadays.'

'I saw something I think might be what you mean,' I told her, 'but it was in the shop called Trends and ruinously expensive, I expect.'

'Well, what's money to you, when I'm going to leave you a million pounds?' she retorted. 'You must do as I ask, or I shall never sleep peacefully again. That girl killed herself, didn't she?'

'I'm afraid so, yes.'

'Then she must not be allowed to *walk*. They do, you know, if precautions are not taken. This is what I want you to do.'

So I bought the doll – it was, as I had anticipated, extremely expensive – and took it to Aunt Eglantine. On the bed was a tangle of wool, some of it black, some of it orange.

'Look here,' I said, 'you don't want to dabble in this kind of thing. Chaucer's Madame Eglantine would never have dreamed of such heathen goings-on.'

'Witchcraft must be met with witchcraft,' said the old lady. 'I hope you cut the holly and did not buy it.'

'Anthony had a tree in his garden.'

'You will have to glue this wool on to the doll's head when I've teased it out a bit more.' I sat silent while her old fingers pulled at and fluffed up the wool. Then she told me what I was to do with the doll, but after my dream, which had been detailed and extraordinarily vivid, I could not face Belas Knap again. I took the box containing the holly-pierced doll to Uley. I did not ask for the key to the long barrow, for the last thing I wanted was to advertise my presence in the neighbourhood on this occasion. I put the box, with the orange-and-black-haired doll in it, under my arm. Then I got out of the car and walked alongside the big field to Hetty Pegler's Tump. I laid the box down on Hetty Pegler's whale-like side and extracted the doll. Then I wondered whether Aunt Eg had intended me to use the box as a coffin (a curious tie-up here with my dream), but, as I doubted whether Neolithic man had concerned himself with coffins, I slung the box and then its lid over the rounded hump of the long barrow and laid the parti-colour-haired doll on the miry ground, wedged up against the wooden door of the burial mound. I knew I should have to lie to Miss Eglantine, but, even if I had had a key to the place, nothing on earth would have induced me to open up and put the pierced body of Gloria Mundy's representative inside that ghost-haunted long barrow.

I trusted that rain and the Cotswold snow would soon do their worst to the doll, and so render it an unacceptable object for any innocent child to pick up and cherish.